Legends of King Arthur

Legends of King Arthur

BY JANYCE L. MINNTON

ILLUSTRATED BY BRUNO FROST

Hart Publishing Company

NEW YORK CITY

Contents

List of Illustrations

Prologue

IN ANCIENT DAYS there lived a noble king called
Uther-Pendragon. And this king became the overlord
of all Britain through the aid and advice of a powerful
enchanter known to all men of the realm as Merlin the
Wise. And Merlin gave unto the mighty monarch
Uther-Pendragon good counsel in affairs and concerns
of state.

Also of very great aid unto Uther-Pendragon was the
very excellent and renowned knight Sir Ulfius, thought
by many to be the greatest leader in war of any man
then alive. And Sir Ulfius gave unto the King aid and
advice in battle. So it came to pass that with the help

of Merlin the enchanter and Sir Ulfius the warrior, Uther-Pendragon overcame all of his enemies.

Now after Uther-Pendragon had ruled his kingdom for some years, he took to wife the beautiful and gentle Lady Igraine, the widow of the Duke of Tintegal. Her two daughters, Margaise and Morgana le Fay, she brought with her to the court of Uther-Pendragon when she did marry that puissant King. But soon afterwards her daughter Margaise was wedded to King Lot of Orkney; and her daughter Morgana le Fay, who was said to be a sorceress, was wedded to King Urien of Gore; and both daughters went away from that court.

Now after some time had passed, a son was born unto Uther-Pendragon and Queen Igraine, and he was very beautiful and of great size and strength of bone. And while the beautiful babe still lay wrapped in his swaddling clothes in his cradle of gold and ultramarine, then came Merlin the enchanter before Uther-Pendragon with the spirit of prophecy strong upon him, and he said:

"Lord, I foresee that thou shalt shortly fall sick of a fever, and mayhap thou shalt not recover. Now should such a dolorous thing befall us all, then this young child will be in very great danger, for assuredly many of your enemies shall rise up to seize him for his inheritance. And it may befall that the child shall be slain, or else he shall be held in captivity for the remainder of his days. And there will be great disorder in the realm when thou art king no more.

"Therefore I do beseech thee, my liege lord, that thou wilt permit Sir Ulfius and myself to carry away the child to some place of safe refuge, where he may be hidden in secret until he groweth to manhood and is able to guard himself from such dangers as threaten him."

"O, Merlin," replied the King in a strong and steady voice, "so far as my death is concerned, I believe God will endow me with the grace to meet my end when my time doth come. For certes my lot is no different from that of any other man. But if thy prophecy be true, then great indeed is my child's danger. Wherefore it would be well that he should be conveyed hence to some place of safe harborage as thou dost advise. But I prithee, dear friend, keep well in mind that he is the most precious inheritance which I bequeath unto my people."

So Merlin and Sir Ulfius took the child away by night, and they told no one where the babe was hidden. And shortly thereafter, Uther-Pendragon was seized with the sickness that Merlin had foretold, and soon he died, as Merlin had foretold.

And after the King's death, it came to pass that all the realm fell into great disorder. Each lesser king contended against his fellows for overlordship, and the land was altogether riven with warfare and strife. Wicked knights and barons harried the highways and

levied heavy tolls upon the hapless. Some travelers they
seized for ransom, and many there were, who not being
ransomed, were slain. And all that dolorous land
groaned with the trouble that lay upon it.

So Merlin and Sir Ulfius took the child away by night

Thus passed nearly eighteen years in great affliction. Then the Archbishop of Canterbury summoned Merlin the enchanter to him in London Town.

And the Archbishop said, "O, Merlin, it is said ye are wise beyond all other men. Can you then not find some means to heal the sorrows of this woeful realm? I pray ye, bend ye your wisdom to this matter and choose a king who shall be a fit overlord for us all, so that once again we may live peaceably as we did in the days of Uther-Pendragon. For the greatest grief that e'er befell this realm was when that King died and left no son to rule after him."

And the spirit of prophecy fell on Merlin, and he replied, "Soon shall this country have a king, and he shall be even wiser and greater than Uther-Pendragon. And he shall bring order and peace where now there is disorder and war."

And the Archbishop said, in glad astonishment, "When is this king to come?"

And Merlin answered, "He will come when ye do call him."

Then the Archbishop said, "Who are his forebears?"

And Merlin answered, "If there is any man of Uther-Pendragon's full blood-royal, it is this man."

"Nay," said the Archbishop, "there is no such man." For he knew nought of the child they had hidden away.

Then he said, "But how shall we know our king when he appeareth among us? For many lesser kings would fain be overlord of this land, and all will claim themselves the rightful king. How shall we know the true King from those others?"

"My lord Archbishop," quoth Merlin, "with your leave I shall set an adventure which if any man achieve it, all the world shall straightway know that he is the rightful king and overlord of this realm."

So by his magic Merlin caused a huge marble stone, four feet square, to appear before the cathedral door. And upon this block of marble there appeared an iron anvil, and thrust into the anvil midway to the hilt was a great sword. And this sword was the most wonderful that any man had ever seen. For the blade was of blue steel, beauteously glittering, and the hilt was of gold, intricately carved and inlaid with many precious stones so that it shone with wondrous brightness in the sunlight. And on the sword was graven in letters of gold:

WHOSO PULLETH OUT THIS SWORD FROM THE ANVIL THAT SAME IS RIGHTWISE KING-BORN OF ENGLAND.

Then Merlin bade the Archbishop that come Christmastide he should call together all the chief people of the land so that every nobleman might assay to draw forth the sword. For he who should succeed in drawing forth that sword from out the anvil would rightwise be acknowledged King of Britain.

Now when the messenger of the Lord Archbishop rode forth across the land, all the people were cast into a great ferment. "Who shall draw forth that sword, and who shall be our King?" they asked. Some thought it would be King Lot and others said it would be King Urien, since both were sons-in-law of Uther-Pendragon; and some thought it would be King Leodegrance of Cameliard; and still others thought it would be King Ryence of North Wales. And all the realm was divided, each man thinking according to his liking.

And when Christmastide drew nigh, it appeared that all the lords and ladies and knights of the realm were wending their way to London Town. And the highways and byways became thick with wayfarers—kings and lords and knights and esquires and pages and men-at-arms. Every inn and castle was filled with travelers, and along the wayside were pitched tents and pavilions for those who could not find shelter.

Now when the Archbishop beheld the multitudes that were assembling, he said to Merlin, "Indeed, it would be singular if among all these kings and noble lords not one should prove to be the true king of this realm."

Unto which Merlin answered, "Marvel not, my lord, if among all those who appear there shall not be found one who is indeed worthy. And marvel not if among all those who are unknown there shall arise one who shall prove himself entirely worthy."

And the Archbishop pondered Merlin's words, and so beginneth this marvelous tale.

The Great Tournament

IT HAPPENED THAT among those worthies summoned to London Town by the Lord Archbishop, there was a certain knight, very honorable and of high estate, named Sir Ector of Bonmaison. And people called him the "Trustworthy Knight" because of the fidelity with which he kept the counsel of those who confided in him and because he performed unto all men, whether of high or low degree, whatsoever he promised to undertake. Therefore was he held in great esteem by all who knew him.

And this noble knight had two sons. Sir Kay was the elder, a young knight of great valor, well renowned for the performance of several achievements in arms. The other was a lad of eighteen years named Arthur who at that time served as Sir Kay's esquire-at-arms.

Accompanied by retainers, esquires, and pages, Sir Ector and his sons came up to London Town and they did take up domicile in a large meadow amid many other noble knights and puissant lords. Here were a multitude of many-colored pavilions, and over each flew the pennant of that lord who dwelt therein. And because of the multitude of pennants, the sky was well-nigh hidden with the fluttering of flags. And the pavilion of Sir Ector was all of green silk, and his banner was emblazoned with a black griffin upon a field of green.

No less than nineteen kings and sixteen dukes were assembled in London Town. And the Archbishop commanded that a stately tournament be held three days before Christmas Day; and to this tournament were bidden all knights of high birth.

Now when Sir Kay did receive news of this tourney, he beseeched his father Sir Ector for permission to enter so that he might bring honor upon his father's house. Then with Sir Ector's consent he did enroll in the list of knights-contestant, and the tourney judges approved his name. And for his esquire-at-arms, Sir Kay chose his brother Arthur to carry his spear and pennant onto the field of battle.

Then on the day of the great tournament, a great

throng of people gathered to behold that courtly assault at arms. No less than twenty thousand lords and ladies were assembled, and so close together were these nobles that they were like a solid wall surrounding the meadow where the battle was to be fought.

Now when all was in readiness, a herald came forward to the throne of the Archbishop. And raising his trumpet to his lips, he blew a mighty blast. And at that signal the gates did open and two parties of knights-contestant entered the meadow, and the green field was all a-glitter with the splendor of sunlight upon the polished armor.

Then did the two parties take their stations, the one at the northern extremity of the field, the other at the southern. And the party with which Sir Kay had cast his lot was at the northern. Numbering fourscore and thirteen, the party of Sir Kay did number three less than the other party; but the party of Sir Kay was nevertheless accounted the stronger, for in its midst were a goodly number of knights famed for great strength and courage.

Now when the contestants had dressed their lances and their shields, the herald blew upon his trumpet yet a second blast. And then did he wait a full minute until all were silent. And then with all his might did he blow a third and final blast.

Upon that note, the two lines of knights rushed forth against each other with such sound and fury that the whole field did groan beneath the feet of the war horses and the very earth itself did tremble.

So the knights clashed in the middle of the field, and the roar of breaking lances was terrible to hear. Then was there great uproar, and the air was filled with the splintered spears of ash wood.

And when the two companies did return unto their stations, the lordly spectators beheld the ground covered with the broken fragments of lances and armor. And many a knight was seen lying in his blood in the midst of all that wreckage. Threescore and ten very noble knights were overthrown, and many were trampled beneath the hoofs of the horses. And some assayed to rise and could not, and others lay quiet as though in death. Then forward ran the pages, and they lifted up the fallen and carried them off to be cared for and healed. Likewise, attendants gathered up the broken armor and the broken spears. And, by and by, the field was clear once more.

Then all those who gazed down upon the meadow gave loud acclaim, for such a noble and glorious contest at arms in friendly assay had never been seen in all that realm.

Now during this assault, none had fought better than Sir Kay. When two opponents charged him at one and the same time, he resisted both spears. And Sir Kay did strike one of those knights with such violence that he fell from horse and rolled over in the dust three times before he lay still.

When the other knights in the party of Sir Kay beheld how he had overthrown that knight, they gave forth with a loud cheer, and Sir Kay was greatly pleased at heart.

Now after the contestants had returned each to his own station, Sir Kay gave Arthur his spear to hold, for the next assault was to be fought with swords. Accordingly when the herald did once again blow upon his trumpet, each knight drew his weapon and a stirring sight it was, to behold those many blades flashing in the sun. And when the herald blew a second time, each knight rode forth to do battle. And immediately there began so fierce a fight that had these knights been bitter enemies, they could not have delivered more vehement blows.

And likewise in this assault did Sir Kay prove so extraordinary that his like was nowhere to be seen in all that field. With great vigor did he strike down five knights.

Upon seeing this, several more knights started toward him in opposition. And among them was Sir Balamorgineas, so huge of frame that he rode head and shoulders above any other man on that field; and of such great strength was he, it was believed he could withstand the assault of three knights at one time.

And when he was nigh to Sir Kay, Sir Balamorgineas

called out, "Ho! ho! Sir Knight of the Black Griffin,
turn thou hither and do battle with me!"

And Sir Kay turned to him, and loudly he retorted,
"I will do battle with thee, and I will cast thee down
as I cast down thy fellows." And he struck with wonderful fierceness at Sir Balamorgineas, so that the mighty
knight was fully bewildered by the blow. His brain felt
so light that he had to hold on to the horn of his saddle
to save himself from falling.

But the fury of that blow did cause the blade of Sir
Kay's sword to snap in half, and it flew high into the
air. And Sir Kay was left without any weapon.

Now Sir Balamorgineas recovered, and seeing his
opponent altogether defenseless, he rushed towards
him. Just then three companions of Sir Kay perceived
his peril, wherefore they thrust themselves between
him and Sir Balamorgineas, and they saved Sir Kay
from being overwhelmed. Then Sir Kay did speedily
make his way through the battle.

As he approached the barrier, young Arthur came
running to him with a goblet of spiced wine. And when
Sir Kay opened the umbril of his helmet to drink, lo!
his face was all covered with sweat, and his throat was
so dry he could hardly speak. And after he had drunk
some wine, his tongue was loosened and he cried out
in violent voice, "Ho! ho! Brother! Get me another
sword. For assuredly would I win much glory for our
house this day."

But the fury of that blow did cause the blade...to snap in half

"But where shall I get thee a sword?" asked Arthur.

And Sir Kay said, "Make haste and fetch me one from our father's pavilion."

So Arthur leaped over the barrier and with all speed ran across the meadow to Sir Ector's pavilion.

But when he came there he found it deserted, for all the people had gone to the field to see the tourney. And search as he might in every corner, he found no sword for his brother.

23

The Miracle of the Sword

NOW ARTHUR was sorely perplexed. As he made his way back to the tournament, of a sudden a thought did spring to his mind! Before the great cathedral, he remembered, he had beheld a sword. Why it stood there, he knew not; nor did he care. But with great excitement, he sped through the twisting streets of London Town until he came before the cathedral. There on a block of marble, embedded in an iron anvil, was the sword.

Straightway Arthur did leap up upon that block of marble and laid his hands unto the hilt of the sword. And he bent his body and drew upon the sword and, lo! it came forth from the anvil with wondrous ease.

Now at the tournament, with great impatience did Sir Kay await the return of Arthur. Wherefore when he finally spied him coming, he vehemently cried out, "Hast got a sword at last?"

"Yea," quoth Arthur, "I have." Whereupon he drew open his cloak.

Now when Sir Kay beheld the sword he knew at once it was the sword from the anvil and he paled and did ask in a strange voice, "Where got ye this sword?"

And Arthur looked upon his brother and beheld that his countenance was greatly disturbed and that his face was white as wax. "Brother, what aileth thee, that thou lookest so strangely?" he said. And he recounted to Sir Kay how he had gotten that sword.

But while Arthur unfolded his tale, Sir Kay did think, "My brother is hardly more than a child, and exceeding innocent is he. He knoweth not what he hath done nor what the doing signifieth. Therefore why should not I claim his achievement and so obtain the kingship?"

Whereupon he said to Arthur, "Give the sword to me. Then betake thyself swiftly unto our father, and bid him come straightway unto the pavilion. And tell no man of this happening."

So Arthur made haste to where Sir Ector sat with the people of his household, and Arthur bade him come, saying, "Truly I think some very extraordinary thing hath befallen my brother for he hath such a countenance as I never saw him wear."

Then Sir Ector marveled greatly that Sir Kay did quit his battle with Sir Balamorgineas and should summon him at such a time. Wherefore he arose and went quickly with Arthur to the pavilion. And in the midst of the tent they beheld Sir Kay with face white as ashes and eyes that shone with a strange brightness.

And Sir Ector cried out, "My son, what aileth thee?"

Whereupon Sir Kay did take his father by the hand and he did lead him to a table whereon lay a cloak all folded over. Thereupon Sir Kay did open the cloak and, lo! within it lay a shining sword. And both hilt and blade glistened with such splendor that Sir Ector knew immediately whence that sword had come.

And written on the sword were these words:

WHOSO PULLETH OUT THIS SWORD FROM THE ANVIL THAT SAME IS RIGHTWISE KING-BORN OF ENGLAND.

And Sir Ector said, "How came you by this sword?"

Then for a moment was Sir Kay silent, but then he spoke out, "Sire, I did break my sword in the battle, whereupon I found me this sword in its stead."

Then said Sir Ector, "If it be thou who didst draw forth this sword from the anvil, then it must be thou who art rightwise King of Britain. But if thou didst indeed draw it forth from the anvil, then shalt thou as easily be able to thrust it back again."

On hearing this, Sir Kay cried out, "Who could do so great a miracle as to thrust a sword into solid iron?"

And Sir Ector replied, "Such a miracle is no greater than the miracle that thou hast already performed when thou didst draw it out."

Now Sir Kay knew not how to answer his father, for he greatly feared that he would be discomforted and found out to be a deceiver. Nevertheless he took what comfort he could, speaking to himself in this wise: "If my young brother Arthur was able to do such a miracle, why should not I command a miracle of a like sort? Assuredly I am no less worthy than he. Wherefore if he drew forth the sword with such ease, it may likewise happen that I, with equal ease, shall thrust it back in place again."

Then Sir Kay wrapped the sword in the cloak again, and he and Sir Ector went forth from the pavilion and made their way to the cathedral. And Arthur followed behind his brother and his father, though they paid him little heed.

And when they came before the cathedral, Sir Kay mounted the cube of marble and beheld the face of the anvil. And, lo! it was altogether smooth and without a scratch or scar. Then was Sir Kay indeed dismayed, but he could not withdraw from that undertaking. Wherefore he set the point of the sword to the anvil and bore down upon it with all his might. But in vain did he labor. For he could not pierce the anvil even to the breadth of a hair.

Then he ceased his endeavor and he walked to where his father stood. "Sire," he said, "no living man can perform that miracle."

And Sir Ector was sorely perplexed. "If thou didst draw out that sword as thou hast said, wherefore canst thou not thrust it back at thy will?"

"My father, have I thy leave to speak?" spoke out young Arthur in a gentle voice.

And Sir Kay turned and sent him forth a dark glance. But Sir Ector replied, "Speak, my son."

And Arthur said, "I would assay to handle that sword."

And Sir Ector quoth, "Wherefore thou?"

"It was I who drew forth that sword from the anvil to replace my brother's sword," said Arthur. And he spoke full sorrowfully, for he did not like to show his brother for a liar. "And if, as thou sayest, to thrust it back is not more difficult than to draw it forth, then I would fain assay the thrusting back."

Then did Sir Ector look so strangely upon Arthur that the boy cried out, "Sire, why dost thou look at me in this way? For I never meant to anger thee."

"God be my witness," quoth Sir Ector, "thou hast not angered me. And if thou dost desire to handle the sword, assuredly thou must."

So young Arthur took the sword from his brother Kay, and he leaped up upon the marble stone. And he set the point of the sword upon the anvil, and he bore strongly upon it and, lo! the sword penetrated smoothly and easily into the center of the anvil until it stood midway deep therein, and there it stood fast. And after he had performed that miracle, he drew forth the sword again easily and swiftly; and then once more he thrust it back into the anvil.

Now when Sir Ector beheld what Arthur did, he cried out, "Lord! Lord! what miracle is this!" Then

Arthur stepped down from the marble cube, and that noble knight Sir Ector did kneel down before him, and Sir Ector set his two hands together palm to palm.

"My father! Wherefore dost thou kneel down to me?" cried Arthur, like one in a great measure of pain.

"Arthur! Now must I needs tell ye that I am not your father," said Sir Ector.

Then Arthur fell a-weeping, saying, "Father, I beseech thee to arise and not to kneel to me."

So Sir Ector arose from his knees, and he stood up before Arthur and he said, "Arthur, why dost thou weep?"

"Because, my lord, I am sore afraid."

"Have no fear," said Sir Ector. "Now is the time for thee to know thyself, for the true circumstances of thy life have heretofore been hidden from thee. But now I may tell thee everything.

"Eighteen years ago there came to me a certain man, very wise and high in favor with Uther-Pendragon, and that man was the enchanter Merlin. And Merlin showed me the signet ring of Uther-Pendragon, and he commanded me by virtue of that ring to come at midnight of that very day to the postern gate of the king's castle.

"Now when I came to the postern gate at midnight, there came unto me Merlin and one man more. And this other man was Sir Ulfius, then chief knight of the household of Uther-Pendragon.

"And Merlin bore in his arms a thing wrapped in a scarlet mantle. And when he opened the folds of the mantle, lo! I beheld a new-born child wrapped in swaddling clothes. Thou, Arthur, wert that child.

"Then did Merlin command me to take that child and to rear him as mine own. And it was Merlin who named that child Arthur; and Merlin commanded me that no one in all the world was to know that that child was not mine own.

"Whereupon I took the child away with me and I said it was mine own, and all the world so knew it. And when that good lady who was my wife died, she took that secret with her to Paradise.

"Nor did I ever learn thy rightful father, but now mayhap I have learned it. For who but the son of Uther-Pendragon could have performed the miracle of the sword?"

When Sir Ector's tale was told, Arthur took again to weeping, and he cried, "Woe! Woe!"

And the knight quoth, "Wherefore such sorrow?"

And honest young Arthur replied, "Because now I have lost my father. For I would rather have my father than be king!"

Now as they were speaking, there appeared before the cathedral two men, each very tall and of a noble stature. And Sir Ector knew these men, for they were Sir Ulfius and the enchanter Merlin.

And Merlin said, "What cheer?"

"Here is cheer of a wonderful sort," said Sir Ector. "For behold, Merlin! here is that child that thou didst bring to me these eighteen years ago and, lo! he hath grown to his manhood."

Then quoth Merlin, "I know him well, for unbeknownst to you, I have watched continually over him. I know what he hath done today, and I know what thou hast told him. And I avouch that thou hast said the truth.

"And high and kingly blood runneth in his veins, and in this young lad lieth the hope and the salvation of Britain. Therefore, care ye tenderly for him, Sir Ector, for in three days' time all the world shall know who he is."

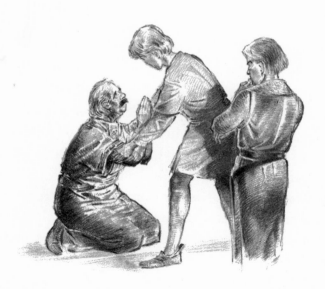

The Mighty Fail

ON THE MORNING of Christmas Day, the sun shone forth bright and clear, and at an early hour there gathered before the great cathedral many thousands of folk of all qualities, both gentle and simple, to behold the assay of the sword. Missing only were Sir Ector and Sir Kay and Arthur, for Merlin had bidden those three to stay in their pavilion until such time as he deemed fit for their coming forth.

Now above the sword and the anvil was spread a multi-colored embroidered canopy, and around the great cube of marble stone a platform had been built. And next to that place had been established a throne for the Archbishop of Canterbury. For the Archbishop himself was to overlook that assay and to guard that every circumstance be filled with due equity.

When the morning was half gone by, the Archbishop came forth with pomp and pageantry, and he did take his seat upon the high throne, and all his court of clerks and knights were gathered about him.

Then did the Archbishop of Canterbury command his herald to sound loud the trumpet, bidding all who were deemed worthy to make assay at the adventure of this sword that Merlin had summoned up.

And unto that assay had gathered nineteen kings and sixteen dukes. And each was possessed of noble and exalted estate, and each hoped that on that day he would be proved the rightwise King and overlord of Britain.

Now immediately the trumpet sounded, the first of those kings appeared and he was King Lot of Orkney. And eleven knights and five esquires stood by in escort, and they made a noble and courtly retinue. And two esquires aided King Lot to mount the platform, and then King Lot saluted the Archbishop, as was fitting. Then in the sight of all, he laid his hands to the pommel of the sword, and he bent his body and he drew upon the sword with great force. But strain as he might, not by so much as a hair's breadth did the sword move. And that sword stayed steadfast in the anvil.

And after that first assay, King Lot made assay three times more, and still he was altogether unsuccessful. Then he ceased his endeavor and he came down from the platform, and he was filled with great anger and shame because he had failed.

And after King Lot, his brother-in-law King Urien of Gore made assay. And he, too, strived valiantly to wrest the sword from its bed, but neither was it given unto him to succeed.

And after King Urien there came King Fion of Scotland, and after King Fion came King Mark of Cornwall, and after King Mark came King Ryence of North Wales, and after King Ryence came King Leodegrance of Cameliard, and after him came all those other noble kings and dukes, but not one could coax that blade to yield up its seat in the anvil.

And all the people who witnessed that adventure were greatly astonished. "How is this?" they asked of one another. "If these exalted kings and dukes have failed to achieve this adventure, may there be any man in the realm who will succeed? For here have come all who are most worthy of this noble task. Is there now to come one still *more* worthy?"

Likewise those kings and dukes spoke together. And by and by, six of the most worthy—to wit, King Lot, King Urien, King Pellinore, King Ban, King Ryence, and Duke Clarence of Northumberland—came before the throne of the Archbishop and they spoke to him in this wise:

"Sire, all the kings and dukes of this realm have striven before you and, lo! not one hath succeeded in this undertaking. Wherefore we six understand that the enchanter Merlin hath set this adventure to bring shame and discredit upon us and even upon you who are the head of the church of this realm. For it hath been demonstrated that no man can draw forth a sword-blade from a bed of solid iron. Therefore we ask you, is it not plain that Merlin hath made a mock of us all?

"And therefore, whilst this great congregation is
still assembled here, we beseech you of your wisdom
to choose from among the kings here gathered that
one who is best fitted to be overlord of this realm. And
whomsoever ye shall choose, him will we promise to
obey in all things. For verily it is foolish and impos-
sible to draw forth a sword from an iron anvil. But it
is wise and reasonable that the Archbishop of Canterbury should choose a king."

Then was the Archbishop much troubled in spirit,
and he pondered privately, "Surely Merlin hath not
deceived me. Nay, Merlin is passing wise, nor would
he make a mock of all the realm for an idle jest. Certes
he hath some intent of which we know naught, being
of less wisdom than he."

Then aloud to those six high lords he said, "Messires,
I pray your patience, and I bid ye wait with me a little
while. But if within the time a man may count five
hundred twice over, no other cometh forward to perform this assigned task, then I will agree that Merlin
hath deceived us. And I will, as you request, choose one
amongst you and proclaim him King and overlord of
Britain."

Whereupon the Archbishop summoned a page, and
that page stood before the sword in the anvil, and he
commenced to count aloud.

Rightwise King
of the Realm

IT BEING TIMELY, now did Merlin and Sir Ulfius go away from the cathedral and they went to the pavilion of Sir Ector. And Merlin said, "The hour hath come for Arthur to stand before the world and do publicly that which he did of late in private." So Arthur arose and came forth from the pavilion with his father and his brother and, lo! he was like one who walked in a dream.

Then the five went down and when they came near the cathedral, the people did make way for them, marveling greatly and saying to one another, "Who are these three with Merlin the enchanter and with Sir Ulfius, and whence come they?" And one man knew Sir Ector and another knew Sir Kay, but all the people said, "Who is that youth that walketh in the middle?"

But Merlin spake no word to any man, and he led Arthur straight through the throng unto the Archbishop's throne. And the page that had been counting hushed, though he had only gotten to five hundred and five and fifty.

And Merlin said, "My lord, here is one come to make the assay of yonder sword."

"By what right doth this young man come hither?" said the Archbishop.

And Merlin said, "He cometh by the best right in the world, for he is the true son of Uther-Pendragon and of his lawful wife Queen Igraine."

Then did the Archbishop cry out in great amazement, and all those who heard the words of Merlin were so astonished that they knew not what to think. And the Archbishop said, "Ye mock me, Merlin. For in all the world, no one hath ever heard that Uther-Pendragon begat a son."

"Indeed very few have known this thing," said Merlin. And then Merlin told the Archbishop and all that assembly how he had foreseen the death of the noble King and how he had saved the child from his father's enemies and how he had given him to Sir Ector to rear as his own child.

And Sir Ulfius and Sir Ector attested to the truth thereof.

Then quoth the Archbishop, "No man may doubt such honorable witnesses." And he looked kindly upon young Arthur and he smiled.

And Arthur said, "Lord, have I your leave to handle yonder sword?"

"Thou hast my leave," said the Archbishop. "May the grace of God go with thee in thy endeavor."

Thereupon Arthur mounted the platform that surrounded the cube of marble and he laid his hands upon

the hilt of the sword. And he bent his body and drew and, lo! the sword yielded with great ease. And when he had altogether freed that noble sword from the anvil, he held it high and commenced to swing it about his head so that it flashed like lightning all about.

And after he had swung it three times about his head, he set the point against the face of the anvil and he bore down upon it. And lo! the sword slid back smoothly into that place where it had stood, and when it was midway deep in the anvil, it held fast. Thus did

*...he swung...the sword...three times about
his head*

young Arthur do the miracle of the sword before the
eyes of all the marveling world.

Then the people lifted up their voices and they gave
forth with a cheer so great that the earth rocked with
their shouting.

And while they shouted, Arthur once more took
hold of the sword and he drew it forth and he swung
it round and he drove it back again into the anvil. And
then again he drew it forth and swung it round and
thrust it back. And all those who were assembled there

beheld that miracle done three times over.

Now all those kings and dukes were sorely perplexed that a slender youth should succeed where they had failed. And some gladly acknowledged Arthur because of that miracle, but others withdrew themselves and stood aloof, saying among themselves, "Should a beardless boy be set before us? And should he be our King? Nay! Nay! we will have none of him over us. For it is plain that Merlin and Sir Ulfius have elevated this unknown boy solely in order that they may themselves be elevated with him." Thereupon with angry and averted faces, a certain number of kings went away from that place, their hearts scalded by wrath. And among these discontented kings the most bitter were King Lot and King Urien, though they were by marriage brothers to Arthur. And others who departed hence were King Ban and King Ryence and King Pellinore and Duke Clarence of Northumberland.

But other kings and dukes came forth and saluted Arthur and paid him gracious court. And chief among those who came forward in friendliness was King Leodegrance of Cameliard. And all the multitude acknowledged Arthur and the people crowded round him, and they cheered and shouted.

But Sir Ector and Sir Kay stood apart from the joyous throng, and they were greatly weighed down by sorrow. For young Arthur had been lifted far above them, and they feared that never more might they approach him. For Arthur was King of the realm, and they but common knights.

Now when Arthur beheld them in such melancholy he went to them straightway, and he took first Sir Ector by the hand and then Sir Kay, and he kissed each upon the cheek. Wherefore that man and his son were uplifted and glad.

And when Arthur departed from the cathedral, great crowds of people followed after him so that the streets were altogether filled with the joyous mobs, and those who were nearest to Arthur sought to touch the hem of his garments. And the multitude continually gave him loud acclaim as the chosen King of England, and they shouted, "Long live King Arthur! Long live England!" Wherefore was young Arthur's heart overfilled with joy and happiness, and his soul sang within him.

That night, a mighty wind blew out of the north. And it wafted up the magic sword and its anvil as if they had been but two feathers, and the wind bore them speedily away.

And Merlin said, "They are gone to the magic isle of Avalon, and no man shall e'er see them again. And there is no sword mightier than that sword, save one —only the sword Excalibur, which men shall see anon, so soon as its owner fetches it."

One Hundred Shields

SOME MONTHS DID pass; and early one spring morn there rode forth from the court at Camelot a noble figure clad all in silver armor and mounted on a milk-white horse. And those who saw him did marvel at the changes that had come about. For, lo! this fair knight who rode forth into the countryside, his spirit bubbling like a young tree with new sap, was none other than King Arthur. But no longer was he the boy monarch with enemies on every side, for now did he reign the absolute and undisputed overlord of the realm.

For young Arthur had been engaged in two great wars, and he had so overthrown his enemies, even his brothers-in-law King Lot and King Urien, that ne'er again would they rise up to challenge Arthur's birthright and authority. And King Ban and Duke Clarence of Northumberland were two others that he overcame, and King Arthur made a peace with them. And King Pellinore he drove off into the forests, and King Ryence he drove into the mountains of North Wales.

Wherefore, with the winning of the famous battle at Bedegraine, there came unto the land such peace the like of which had not been enjoyed since the days of Uther-Pendragon.

Thus was the reign of King Arthur entirely established, and his greatness was spoken of everywhere, and there gathered about the King at Camelot young men of noble spirit and knightly rank. And these knights desired above all other things to achieve glory at arms in courts of chivalry, for they sought exaltation of estate from their King.

Therefore did these brave young knights now roam the countryside in search of adventures wherein they might champion justice and prove each his courage, his courtesy, and his prowess. In like manner on that spring day did King Arthur leave behind him the burden of kingly matters and himself rode forth in search of knightly adventure.

And indeed a very pleasant thing it is to ride forth in the dawning of a springtime day. For it is then that the little birds do sing their sweetest, joining all in one joyous medley, wherefore one may scarce tell one note from another, so multitudinous is that pretty roundelay. And then it is, in the freshness of the early daytime, that the growing things of the earth do smell the sweetest. Then is all the sward of the earth—the fair flowers, the shrubs, and the blossoms upon the trees—with dew bespangled as with a multitude of jewels. Then is all the world sweet and clean and new, as though it had been fresh created for him who cometh early in the morning to roam abroad.

Therefore King Arthur's heart did expand with joy, and he chanted a quaint song as he rode through the forest in quest of knightly adventure.

Now of a sudden there appeared in that forest a sad and woeful sight. Betwixt the trees came a knight sore wounded, and he was supported upon his horse by a golden-haired page. And the knight's face was as pale as wax, and his head fell forward as if he were sleeping, and his eyes were glazed so that he saw naught of what passed before him, and his apparel of white and blue was all stained red with the blood of life that ran from a great wound in his side.

Now as he witnessed the approach of these sorry two, King Arthur cried out, "Alas! what doleful spectacle is this? I prithee tell me, Page, who is thy master? And how came he to such a sad and pitiable condition?"

"My lord," replied the youth, "my master here is Sir Myles of the White Fountain and he cometh from the north country. A fortnight hence, moved by the lustiness of springtime, he set forth with no escort save myself, who am his esquire. For Sir Myles had a mind to seek adventure in such manner as befitteth a good knight. And indeed several adventures did we have, and in all of them was my lord successful.

"But this morning came we upon a stone bridge that led to a lonesome castle. And before this solitary castle stood a wondrous thing—an apple tree hung over with a hundred shields. And midway upon that stone bridge was a single shield entirely of black, and beside the shield hung a hammer of brass, and beneath the shield was written for all to see in letters of red:

WHOSO SHALL SMITE THIS SHIELD
DOETH SO AT HIS PERIL.

"Now my master Sir Myles, when he did read those forbidding words, went straightway to that shield and, seizing the hammer that hung beside it, he smote a blow so mighty that it rang like thunder.

"Whereupon at once the portcullis of the castle was let fall, and forth rode a knight clad all from head to foot in sable armor, and all the trappings of his horse were likewise of sable, all black and unmottled.

"Then did that Sable Knight come riding swiftly across the meadow and over the bridge, and he drew rein and saluted my master, and he cried out, 'Where-fore didst smite that shield? Now know thou that because of thy boldness, I shall take away from thee thine own shield, and I shall hang it upon yonder tree with all those others.'

"And my master replied, 'That shalt thou not do, unless knight to knight thou overcomest me.'

"Then did my master and this Sable Knight make ready for encounter, and they came at each other with might and main. And, alas! in the middle of the course, my master's spear burst into splinters. But the spear of the Sable Knight held, and it pierced through my master's shield and through his side, and both he and his horse were violently overthrown. And Sir Myles' wound was so grievous that he could not arise from the ground whereon he lay.

"Then did the Sable Knight take my master's shield and he hung it from the apple tree with the other shields, and with no further heed to my master and without inquiring as to his hurt, away he rode into his castle and the portcullis was immediately closed behind him."

"By the glory of Paradise!" cried King Arthur, "what discourtesy to leave a fallen knight upon the ground and to take away the shield of one who hath done good battle! Forsooth, I will humble that Sable Knight, and not only for mine own honor, but to avenge the honor of Sir Myles and those other knights as well. Wherefore I prithee tell me, lad, where groweth this infamous apple tree?"

Whereupon the page did point northward with his finger, and King Arthur set spurs to his horse and he rode off apace to meet his bold adventure.

Now he had not ridden but a mile when he came upon an old man mounted on a palfrey. And that old man was the enchanter Merlin, and Arthur greeted him gladly, saying, "What cheer?"

But Merlin quoth, "Nay, lord, here is no cheer at all, for thou art in great peril. Wherefore do thou bid me ride with thee, for the sake of that danger that I see and thou dost not see."

"Merlin," answered the King, "even were I to face my death, I would not turn back from a noble adventure. But seeing thou hast always been friendly to me, at thy request I take thee with me."

Whoso shall smite this shield doeth so at his peril.

The Sable Knight

AND KING ARTHUR and Merlin rode northward
through the dark forest for a considerable while, until they approached the dwelling-place of the Sable
Knight. Before them lay a dark and dismal glen, and
through that glen a stream rushed with great violence.
A bridge of stone crossed over that stream, and upon
the far side of the bridge was planted a smooth and
level lawn of grass whereon two knights-contestant
might well joust. And beyond this lawn there rose up
a tall and forbidding castle with smooth walls and a
straight tower, and this castle was so built upon the
rocks that it did seem verily part of the stone.

And just as the page of Sir Myles had said, midway
upon the bridge they beheld a single black shield and
a hammer of brass; and before the castle stood an apple
tree, and one hundred shields, each different one from
the other, were hung among the leaves of that tree.
Now some of those shields were clean and fair, and
some were foul and stained with blood; some were
smooth and unbroken, and some were cleft by battle.
And all those hundred shields had been taken in combat by the Sable Knight.

"Splendor of Paradise!" exclaimed King Arthur. "Forsooth that must be a most valiant knight who hath cast down so many other knights."

And Merlin said, "Yea, my lord. Wherefore seest thou that thy shield shall not hang there too, ere the sun goeth down this eventide."

To which with a steadfast countenance King Arthur did reply, "That shall be as God willeth. But certes I am of greater mind than ever to try my hand against yon Sable Knight, for in truth great honors would be rightly rendered me were I to overcome so worthy a knight."

Thereupon King Arthur spurred his horse forward to the bridge, and there he read the challenge that was written in letters of red beneath the shield:

WHOSO SHALL SMITE THIS SHIELD
DOETH SO AT HIS PERIL.

Then straightway the King seized the brazen hammer and he delivered a royal blow upon that shield, and the sound echoed back from the smooth walls of the castle and from the rocks whereon it stood and even from the edge of the forest beyond.

Whereupon in answer to that sound, the portcullis of the castle was let fall, and forth did ride a knight huge of frame and clad from head to foot in sable armor. And the trappings of his horse were also of sable, so that this knight did present a most grim and forbidding aspect. Then did the Sable Knight come riding across the meadow. And he did not ride in haste, nor did he ride slowly, but he rode forward with great pride and haughtiness, as becometh a champion who never yet hath been vanquished in battle.

Upon reaching the bridge, he drew rein and he saluted King Arthur with great dignity. "Ha! Sir Knight," said he. "Wherefore didst thou defy my caution and smite upon my shield? For thy discourtesy I shall straightway deprive thee of thy shield and I shall hang it upon that apple tree where I have hung a hundred other shields. Therefore, without more ado, yield me thy shield, or else prepare to defend it with thy person!"

"I thank thee for this courteous choice," said King Arthur. "But as for the taking of my shield, I do believe that that shall be as Heaven willeth, and not as thou willest. Know thou, unkind knight, that I have come hither for no purpose other than to do battle with thee and to redeem with my person all those shields that hang upon that tree. Therefore make thyself ready so that I may do with thee as I have sworn."

"So be it," replied the Sable Knight with great scorn. Thereupon he turned his horse, and he rode back a certain distance, and he took his stand in such place as appeared advantageous to him. And likewise King Arthur rode forth onto the meadow to take his station as seemed fit to him.

Then each knight dressed his spear and his shield to do battle, and when both were prepared for combat, each urged forward his war horse and drove his spurs into its flanks.

Then did those two noble steeds rush forth like lightning, coursing across the ground with such speed that the earth did tremble and shake beneath them. And the two knights met fairly in the center of the field, crashing together like a thunderbolt. And so violently did they smite the one against the other that their spears burst into splinters and their horses reeled backward from the force of the collision.

Now King Arthur was much amazed not to have overthrown his opponent, for the King was acclaimed the most worthy knight in all of Britain, wherefore he marveled at the power of the Sable Knight. So when they came together again in the midst of the field, King Arthur gave greeting to the Sable Knight and bespoke him with great courtesy, "Sir Knight, I know not who thou art, but herewith do I pledge my knightly word that thou art the most puissant knight I have ever encountered. Now do I bid thee to dismount straightway from thy horse and do battle on foot with me."

"Not so," quoth the Sable Knight, "not so. Not until the one or the other of us be overthrown will I contest this battle upon foot."

Then in a very loud voice he shouted, "Ho! Ho!" Whereupon the gates of the castle swung open, and

forth ran two esquires clad all in black. And each esquire bore in his hand a great spear of ash wood, new
and well seasoned and never before wielded in battle.

Then King Arthur chose one of these spears and the
Sable Knight took the other, and they returned each
to his station. Then once again each knight did rush
his steed to the assault, and once again each smote the
other so fairly in the midst of his defense that both
spears were completely shattered, and each knight was
left with only the guard and the truncheon in his grasp.

Then, as before, did King Arthur offer to fight the
battle with swords and upon foot, but this time, too,
the Sable Knight would have none of it. Thereupon
he called out once more to the esquires within the
castle, and forth they came again with spears for the
warriors. So each knight, having again armed himself,
returned to his station upon that fair meadow.

And now for the third time those two most excellent knights did hurl themselves at each other in furious
assault. And yet again, as twice before, King Arthur
did strike the Sable Knight so fairly in the center of
his defense that the spear which Arthur held burst all
to splinters.

But this time the spear of the Sable Knight did not
break. Indeed, so powerful was the blow that he delivered upon King Arthur's shield that his spear pierced
through its very center. And at that same moment, the
girths of the King's saddle burst apart, and both he and

his steed were cast violently backward. And King
Arthur would have been laid low had he not voided his
saddle with extraordinary skill. Though his horse was
thrown to the ground, Arthur himself gained his footing and did not fall. Nonetheless, so violent was the
blow that he received that for some little while everything did whirl before his eyes.

When he had recovered his sight, King Arthur was
so overcome with anger and remorse that the blood in
his heart rushed to his brains so that he saw naught
but red before his eyes. And when this condition passed,
he perceived that the Sable Knight sat upon his horse
at no great distance. Immediately then did King
Arthur run up to him, and catching the bridle rein of
his horse, he cried out, "Dismount, thou black knight,
and engage me with thy sword upon foot."

"That I shall not do," said the Sable Knight, "for,
lo! I have fairly overthrown thee. Therefore deliver
up to me thy shield to hang on yonder apple tree.
Then go thy way as the others have done before thee."

A Fierce Battle Waged

UPON HEARING this insulting command, King Arthur exclaimed with passion, "On my life, sir! neither will I yield myself nor will I go hence until either thou or I have altogether conquered the other." Thereupon he did so vehemently grasp the bridle rein of the other that the Sable Knight was in need to void his saddle to save himself from being thrown upon the ground.

And now was each knight furious. Standing face to face, each drew his sword and dressed his shield, and they did rush together in battle like two mad bulls. Again and again did they feint, smite, trace, and parry. And as they struck again and once again, the sound of their blows crashing and clashing filled the air with a fearsome din. Such was the fury of this affray that whole cantels of armor were hewn from their bodies, and deep and grievous were the wounds received, and the armor of each was altogether red-stained with blood.

So did they battle for some time until King Arthur, like one who has taken leave of his senses, struck upon the other a blow so fierce that no armor could withstand it. But alas! his mighty sword broke at the hilt and the blade flew into the air, while the Sable Knight did groan and stagger and run about in a circle as though blind.

But presently that knight recovered, and casting aside his damaged shield, he grasped his sword with both hands. Therewith he dealt the King so weighty a blow that he clave through King Arthur's shield and through his helmet and even to the bone of his brain-pan.

And now it seemed to the King that he had gotten his death-wound, for his brains were as thin as water, and his thighs trembled. Blood and sweat mingled inside his helmet and flowed down into his eyes and blinded his vision. And the King sank down onto his knees.

Seeing that splendid knight so grievously hurt, the Sable Knight beseeched Arthur to yield himself and to surrender up his shield. And indeed King Arthur seemed too weak to fight any more, and a lesser knight would needs have succumbed. But that valorous king would not yield, and catching the other by his sword belt, he did lift himself up onto his feet. Then, being in a manner somewhat recovered, he did encircle his enemy from behind with both arms, and lifting him aloft he cast the Sable Knight down upon the ground. With such force did the Sable Knight strike the earth that immediately his senses did leave him.

Then straightway did King Arthur unlace the helm

of the Sable Knight, and through the blood that flowed continually down his face, the King did distinguish the countenance of that noble knight. And, lo! that knight was none other than King Pellinore, who had been driven away after the Battle of Bedegraine.

"Ha! Pellinore, is it then thou?" quoth the King. "Now yield thyself unto me, for thou art entirely at my mercy." And so saying, he drew his misericorde and placed the point at King Pellinore's throat.

But King Pellinore had recovered from his fall, and perceiving the blood that still flowed from the other's helmet, he knew that his enemy was sorely wounded. Wherefore did he grasp King Arthur's wrist with his hand and he turned the point of the dagger away from his own throat and toward the throat of the King.

And indeed King Arthur was now exceeding faint from loss of blood. Wherefore it took but scant strength for Pellinore to heave himself suddenly from the ground and to overthrow his enemy, so that now Arthur lay beneath the other's knees.

And the eyes of the Sable Knight were all beshot with blood like unto the eyes of a wild boar, and a froth like the champings of a wild boar stood in his beard about his lips. And mad with the fury of battle, he wrenched the dagger from Arthur's hand and set himself to unlace the King's helm, for he did verily intend to slay him.

Now from the cover where he had stood witness

. . . he turned the point of the dagger . . . toward the
throat of the King.

did Merlin rush forward, crying out, "Stay! Stay, Sir Pellinore! For he who lieth beneath you is your over-lord, and he is Arthur, King of all this realm!"

Astonished beyond measure, for a moment was King Pellinore silent. Then quoth he in choler, "Say you so, old man? Verily your words have doomed this royal knight to death. For in all this world no man hath suffered such ill as I have suffered at the hands of King Arthur. For, lo! he hath taken from me power, and kingship, and honors, and estates, and hath left me with only this gloomy castle. Therefore, if this is he who lieth here in my power, I needs must make an end of him. For were I to let him free, some worse re-venge would he surely wreak on me when he hath recovered from his wounds."

"Nay, Sir Knight," quoth Merlin. "When Arthur dieth, it shall not be at your hands." Whereupon he lifted up his staff and he touched King Pellinore across the shoulders. And at once, like one who has suddenly departed life, the Sable Knight did fall down upon his face, quiet upon the ground.

Encounter in the Forest

SOON AFTER, King Arthur lifted himself somewhat and beheld his enemy lying as though dead. Then he cried out in scorn of Merlin, "What hast thou done! Now hast thou grieved me sorely. For I do perceive that by thy arts of magic thou hast slain one of the most noble knights in all the world."

"Not so, my lord," quoth Merlin. "It is thou who art nigh to death, and not this knight. Pellinore is but in sleep and will soon awaken, but thou art sore wounded and I fear for thee."

Indeed the life seemed to be running fast from that noble king, and it was only with much travail and force of will that Arthur could get up upon his horse. Then, having hung the King's shield upon the horn of his saddle, and leaving the valiant Pellinore where he lay, Merlin mounted his palfrey, and he did guide the King's horse and its wounded rider across the bridge and into the forest. And that royal knight was all bloody and broken.

And those two wandered through the woods until nightfall, and they came to the sanctuary of a holy hermit. Now this hermit did dwell so deep in the forest that when he rang his bell for matins or for vespers only the wild creatures could hear the sound, for no men dwelt anywhere thereabouts. But despite the desolation of that place, betimes noblemen and others would come in pilgrimage to pay homage to this saintly man.

Thither did Merlin convey the wounded Arthur, and lifting down that woeful king from his saddle they carried him into a cave, wherein they laid that royal knight upon a bed of moss. Then they did remove his armor and bathed his wounds and dressed his hurts, but all their ministrations seemed to no avail, for Arthur lay like one nigh unto death. And for all that day and part of the next his breath did flutter, and his head did swim, and his eyes beheld visions of eternity.

Now the next afternoon that quiet forest did suddenly commence to ring with noise and tumult. For the Lady Guinevere, the daughter of King Leodegrance of Cameliard, was come upon a pilgrimage to that holy man. Her favorite page was sick with a ghastly fever, and that fair lady was in hope that the saintly man might have some amulet wherewith to heal him.

With Guinevere had come all her court of ladies and knights, so that the silence of the forest gave way to the merry sounds of speech and laughter and the singing of songs and the neighing of horses. And in the midst of her court rode the lady herself, and her beauty outshone the beauty of her damsels as the morning star outshines the lesser stars. For, then and ever afterward, the Lady Guinevere was held by all the courts of chivalry to be the most beauteous damsel in all this world.

Then to Merlin did she address herself. "O, father, to whom belongeth that noble steed that grazeth yonder?"

And Merlin replied, "Kind lady, the master of that horse is a most noble knight, but now he lieth quiet within that cell so sorely wounded that he is nigh unto death!"

And the lady said, "I do beseech ye lead me to him, for I have in my court a most skillful leech, for though fevers do puzzle him, in healing such hurts as knights receive in battle he hath no peer."

Whereupon Merlin led the lady into the cave, and she beheld King Arthur upon his pallet. And she knew not that he was King, yet it did seem to her that ne'er in all her life had she beheld so noble a knight as this. Now on the sudden King Arthur cast up his gaze, and in the great weakness that lay upon him verily he did not know if he beheld a mortal lady or mayhap some angel mercifully come down from Paradise to minister to him in his pain.

And Lady Guinevere was filled with pity at his sorrowful state. Whereupon she summoned her leech, and she bade him bring precious balsam, and she commanded him to search the knight's wounds and to anoint them with balm.

And that wise and skillful leech did as his lady commanded and, lo! soon was King Arthur relieved of dolor, and his aches were wondrously lessened. And he was much uplifted in heart and mind, and three days after the departure of the Lady Guinevere and her court, Arthur was wholly healed and he was as well and strong as ever he had been.

And from the moment that King Arthur beheld Lady Guinevere she lived constantly in his thoughts. Wherefore King Arthur did swear, "Henceforth I will cherish this lady, and I will serve her as faithfully as ever a worthy knight did serve his chosen dame."

The Lady of the Lake

NOW THAT HE was healed of these grievous wounds, King Arthur did desire most earnestly to challenge Pellinore again. But when he had confided his wish to Merlin, that sage did reply, "Surely thou art the bravest of men to have so keen an appetite for battle, knowing how nigh thou camest to thy death. Yet how mayest thou hope to undertake this adventure? For, lo! thou hast no sword, nor hast thou a spear, nor hast thou even thy misericorde!"

"Then," quoth the King, "I will seek another weapon. And even if I own but an oaken cudgel, yet do I swear I will again assay battle with that powerful knight."

"If thou art indeed fixed in thy purpose," quoth Merlin, "and art sworn to it, I will aid thee as best I can.

"Now in a certain part of this forest, there is a woodland that some call Arroy. But others call it the Forest of Adventure, for no knight doth enter there but some adventure doth befall him. And close unto Arroy there lieth a land of enchantment wherein doth lie a wide and considerable lake, and that lake likewise is enchanted. For in the center of that lake there doth appear from time to time a woman's arm clad in white samite and exceeding beautiful. And the hand of this arm doth hold up a sword, and this sword is the most excellent sword in all the world. And the name of this sword is Excalibur.

"Now know thou that many knights have endeavored to obtain Excalibur for their own, but heretofore not one hath succeeded even to touch it, and many have lost their lives in that adventure. For when any man draweth near to that sword, either he doth sink into the lake or else the arm that holdeth the sword doth disappear.

"So if this adventure pleaseth thee, I will conduct thee to that enchanted lake, and thou mayest behold Excalibur with thine own eyes. For truly, my lord, shouldst thou procure it, thou wilt have a sword quite fitted for battle—indeed, thou wilt have a sword fit for a king!"

"Yea," quoth King Arthur, "I fain would assay to possess that sword. Wherefore I beseech thee, lead me with all haste to that enchanted lake."

And Merlin said, "Yet I have told thee men have died in that assay."

"Nay," quoth King Arthur, "mayhap I shall not die. But if I go forth to Pellinore without that sword, thou knowest I shall surely die."

And on that very morn did King Arthur and the enchanter Merlin take leave of that saintly hermit, and they commenced to wend their way into the depths of the forest. At noontide they did enter into that forest called Arroy, and they came in time to a certain open place where they did spy a doe of the purest white, and about its neck was fastened a golden collar. And King Arthur said, "Let us follow this pretty doe." Then straightway the doe turned about, and Merlin and Arthur followed.

By and by, the twain did arrive at an opening in the trees, and they beheld a glade of sweet, soft grass. Therein was a bower, and before that bower was a table spread with a snow-white cloth and set with refreshment of white bread and wine and meats. At the door of this bower stood a page clad all in green, and his hair was as black as ebony and his eyes were black as jet. And this page greeted them most pleasantly, saying, "King Arthur, ye are welcome."

Now King Arthur was much astonished that here so deep in the forest a page should know him well, and he was fearful lest some enchantment be at work against him. But Merlin bade him have good cheer, saying, "My lord, meseems this refreshment was prepared especially for thee."

So King Arthur sat down to table and was much comforted for he was exceedingly hungry. And that page and yet another did minister to his needs, serving him food upon plates of silver and serving him wine in goblets of gold. So was he indeed served in his own court, but the furniture here in this bower was e'en more cunningly wrought than that at Camelot.

Now when King Arthur had taken his fill and had washed his hands from a silver basin and had dried his hands upon fine linen, he and Merlin betook themselves hence. And they rejoiced greatly at the pleasant adventure which had befallen them. Such a happening, it seemed to the King, could not but betoken a good issue for his undertaking.

So in mid-afternoon the twain went forth from the woods and came out onto a fair and level plain all covered with flowers.

And indeed a wondrous land was this for, lo! all the air appeared to be dusted with gold, so bright was the landscape and so marvelously radiant. Here and there upon that plain were sundry trees all in blossom, and the fragrance of the blooms was sweeter than any the King had ever known. And in the branches of those trees were a multitude of many-colored birds.

And midway in this sweet plain was a lake with water bright as silver, and all around its borders grew lilies and daffodils in great number. But nowhere was there sign of man, and that plain appeared as lonely as a hollow sky upon a summer's day.

And because of the beauty of that place and its solitude, King Arthur perceived he had come unto a land of powerful enchantment. Therefore he urged his milk-white steed through the grass, awaiting whatever strange thing might befall.

Now when he had come to the margin of the lake, he beheld the miracle of which Merlin had told. For, lo! in the midst of that lake there emerged a woman's arm, fair and beautiful, clad in white samite and encircled with bracelets of gold. And the hand held aloft a sword and, behold! the sun shone down upon the hilt of that sword, and the hilt was of pure gold beset with jewels that glistened like unto stars.

Now as King Arthur sat upon his horse and gazed upon the arm and the sword, neither the arm nor the sword moved so much as a hair's breadth, and both remained as motionless as a carven image. And Arthur marveled greatly. Yet he knew not how he might come by that brilliant sword, for the lake was wide and deep.

And as he pondered, suddenly through the tall flowers that bloomed along the margin of that lake he spied a lady approaching. Quickly he dismounted and went forth to meet her. And as he came nigh unto her, he beheld that she was of surpassing beauty, her face as clear as wax and her eyes entirely black. And those eyes glistened in that face like jewels set in ivory. And her black hair was like silk, and so long it reached the ground she walked on. And she was clad all in green, save for a fine cord of crimson and gold that was woven into the plaits of her hair. And around her neck hung a necklace of opals and emeralds set in gold, and around her wrists were bracelets, also of opals and emeralds set in gold.

And King Arthur knelt down before her amid the flowers, and he said, "My lady, I do perceive that ye are no mortal damsel. Methinks ye are a faerie of high and exalted rank and that this glade wherein I stand is some enchanted abode."

"Yea," quoth the lady, "I am indeed fay. And I may tell ye that my name is Nymue, and I am the chiefest of those Ladies of the Lake of whom ye have heard tell. Also ye are to know that yonder seeming lake is, in truth, a plain like unto this one, all covered with flowers. And likewise ye are to know that in the midst of that plain there standeth a castle of white marble and of sky-blue ultramarine, illuminated all about with gold. But so mortal eyes may not behold our dwelling place, my sisters and I did cause this appearance of a lake to extend over all that castle and to hide it entirely from sight. Nor may any mortal man cross that lake, save in one way, else he shall certainly perish."

"My lady, what you tell me doth cause me great wonder. And indeed," said King Arthur, "I fear that I have done amiss in coming hither to intrude upon the solitude of your abode."

"Nay, not so," replied the lady, "for in truth ye are most welcome here. Wherefore I do beseech ye to tell me what purpose bringeth ye to our land."

Whereupon King Arthur did recount to the beautiful Nymue how he had battled with the Sable Knight, and how he had burst his spear and snapped his sword and had even lost his misericorde. And he recounted how he had sworn to fight that knight again, even if an oaken cudgel were all his weapon. And he told her how Merlin had praised the sword Excalibur and how they had come to Arroy to obtain that sword.

"Ha! my lord King," said the Lady of the Lake, "that sword is not easily won. For the man who winneth that sword must be without fear and without reproach."

"Alas!" cried the King. "Methinks I do not lack in knightly courage, yet there are many things for which I do reproach myself. Nevertheless I would assay this adventure, even though it be to my misfortune. Wherefore I pray you, tell me how I may best undertake this assay."

And the lady said, "That will I gladly do." Whereupon she lifted an emerald that hung by a small golden chain from her girdle and, lo! the emerald was carved into the form of a whistle. And she set the whistle to her lips and she did blow shrilly upon it.

Then straightaway there appeared a great way off upon the water a certain thing that shone most brightly. And as it drew near with great speed, behold! it was a boat of carven brass. And the prow of that boat was carved like the head of a beautiful woman, and upon either side were wings like the wings of a swan. And that boat did move upon the water very swiftly like a swan, so that long lines like silver threads stretched after it across the face of the water, which otherwise was like glass for smoothness. And when the brazen boat did reach the bank, it rested there and moved no more.

Then did the Lady of the Lake bid King Arthur enter that boat. And immediately he had done so, the boat moved away from the bank as swiftly as it had come thither. And Merlin and the Lady of the Lake stood upon the margin of the lake and gazed after it.

Then the boat did float across the lake straight to that arm that held the uplifted sword, and all the while the arm and the sword moved not at all.

Now when he came unto the middle of the lake, King Arthur reached forth and grasped Excalibur in his hand, and immediately the arm disappeared beneath the water. But King Arthur held the sword and the scabbard and the belt in his hand and, lo! they were now his own. Then verily his breast did swell with gladness, and his heart was filled with great joy.

Then the brazen boat bore him speedily back to land, and he stepped ashore beside Merlin and the Lady of the Lake. And he gave great thanks to that lady for her aid in this undertaking, and he saluted her. Then mounted he his steed and Merlin mounted his palfrey, and the twain rode off. And that sword, Excalibur, was the most beautiful and the most mighty in all the world.

King Arthur . . . grasped Excalibur in his hand

A Battle Waged
unto Victory

AND THAT NIGHT King Arthur and Merlin did abide once again with the holy man in the forest sanctuary. And when the morning had come, they took their leave, offering thanks to that saintly man for the harborage he had given them.

Anon, about noontide, they reached the valley of the Sable Knight. Here they found all things unchanged from when they first set foot upon that sorrowful strand: to wit, the gloomy castle, the lawn of smooth grass, the apple tree all hung with shields, and that awesome shield of sable with its brass hammer and its dire legend.

"Now, Merlin," quoth Arthur, "this time I do forbid thee to interfere in this affray. And if thou dost assay thy arts of magic in my behalf, then shalt thou suffer my great displeasure."

Thereupon the King rode forth upon the bridge and, seizing the brazen mallet, he smote upon the sable shield. Immediately the portcullis of the castle was let fall and, in the same manner as before, the Sable Knight rode forth, dressed and equipped for encounter. And when they met upon the bridge, King Arthur declared:

"Sir Pellinore, this time we know one another full well, and each doth judge that he hath cause for quarrel: thou, that I have taken from thee thy kingly estates, and have driven thee into this solitude; I, that thou hast set thyself to do injury and affront to knights and lords of my realm. Wherefore, seeing that I do come here as an errant knight, I do challenge thee to do battle with me man to man, until either thou or I have altogether vanquished the other."

In answer to this speech King Pellinore bowed his assent. Then each knight wheeled his horse, and riding back some distance, each took his station where aforetime he had stood. At once there came forth from the castle a tall esquire clad all in sable, and he gave unto King Arthur a good stout spear, well seasoned and untried in battle.

And when the two knights were duly prepared, each shouted aloud and they drove their horses together, the one knight smiting the other so fairly in the midst of his defense that the spears shivered in the hand of each, bursting all into small splinters as they had done aforetime. Then did each knight with great skill and address dismount from his horse, and each drew his sword and fell into combat. And so furious and so violent was their encounter that two wild stallions upon the mountains could not have engaged in more desperate battle.

But now, aided in his cause by his wondrous sword Excalibur, King Arthur soon overcame his rival, delivering unto the Sable Knight grievous wounds, yet he himself was wounded not at all. Nor in all that fight did Arthur shed a drop of blood, but the armor of Pellinore was stained with crimson. Then did Arthur deal the Sable Knight one last vehement and puissant stroke, and Pellinore became as one benumbed, wherefore his sword and his shield fell to the ground, and his thighs trembled beneath him, and he sank unto his knees upon the ground. Then did he beseech King Arthur to have mercy, saying, "My lord and king, I prithee spare my life, and gladly do I yield myself to ye, my liege lord."

And King Arthur said, "Gladly do I spare thee. Nay, I do more than spare thee; for I bear thee no ill-will, Pellinore, and now that thou hast paid me obeisance, I restore unto thee thy power and thy estates. But know thou, Pellinore, that I brook no rebellion in this realm, for as God doth judge me, I do declare that I hold singly in my sight the good of the people of this land. Wherefore he who stands against them also stands against me, and he who stands against me also stands against them."

Then did King Arthur and King Pellinore go together into the castle, where Pellinore's wounds were dressed and his hurts allayed. And King Arthur passed the night in that castle. And on the rising of the next morn, he and Merlin did repair to the court of the King which was at Camelot.

The Magic of Excalibur

NOW AS KING ARTHUR and Merlin rode together through the forest, the King was much pleased. For it was the leafiest time of the year, and the woodlands were bedecked in their best apparel of bright green. Every glade was sweet with the perfume of the thickets, and in every tangle the small bird sang with all his might, so that it seemed his little throat might burst from singing. And the ground was soft with fragrant grass so that where King Arthur and Merlin rode there was no sound of hoofbeats. And the bright yellow sunlight came down through the leaves so that all the ground was scattered o'er as with circles of gold, and the circles trembled in the gentle breeze. And from time to time the sunlight would fall upon the King as he rode, so that his armor seemed to catch fire. Then would his armor shine forth like a bright star amid the dark shadows of the woodland.

And King Arthur took great joy in that forest land, for he was without ache or pain, and his heart was much elated with the success of his adventure.

Now as King Arthur and Merlin rode together through the forest, of a sudden Merlin did ask of the

King, "Which wouldst thou rather have, my liege lord, Excalibur or the sheath that doth hold him?"

To which King Arthur replied, "Ten thousand times would I rather have Excalibur than his sheath."

And Merlin said, "Thou art mistaken. Now of so great a temper is Excalibur that he may cut in twain either a feather or a bar of iron. Yet his sheath is twenty times more precious, for he who weareth it can suffer not a whit from any wound, nor lose a single drop of blood. In witness whereof, thou wilt remember that in thy battle with Pellinore thou didst suffer no wound, neither didst thou lose any blood."

Then the countenance of the King did darken, and he said in great displeasure, "Merlin, thy words have taken from me all the glory of battle. For what credit may be accorded a knight who doth fight his enemy by means of magic? Forsooth, I am minded to take this unearthly sword and to cast it back into that enchanted lake where it belongeth. For a knight should do battle by means of his own strength and not by means of magic."

And Merlin did make reply in this wise, "My liege lord, thou speakest valiantly, albeit not wisely. For thou art no knight errant, but king of the realm, and thy life belongeth not to thyself but to thy people. Therefore thou hast no right to imperil thy life, but must do all that lieth in thy power to preserve it. Wherefore thou must cherish that sword."

And King Arthur did meditate for a while in silence; and then he spoke again, saying, "Verily, I will keep Excalibur to fight with, and for the sake of my people his sheath to preserve my life. Nonetheless, I never will use him again, save only in mortal combat."

And so King Arthur kept Excalibur as his chiefest treasure, and he had made for it a strong chest bound around with many bands of iron and studded all over with iron nails and locked with three great locks. And in this strongbox Excalibur, all wrapped in swathings of fine linen, did lie upon a cushion of crimson silk.

And very few were they who beheld the sword, except at such rare times when in the pitch of battle it shone like a sudden flame. For King Arthur would remove the sword from its bed of silk only to defend his realm from its enemies, and for no other occasion.

But when he had fastened Excalibur to his side, he was like unto a hero armed with a blade of lightning. Yea, at such times Excalibur shone with so fierce a brightness that the very sight of it would overwhelm a wrongdoer with such fear that he would, in a manner, suffer the pangs of death ere ever the edge of the blade had touched his flesh.

And so King Arthur did treasure Excalibur, and the sword remained with him throughout his life. Wherefore are the name of Arthur and of Excalibur as one.

The Enchanted Island

NOW KING ARTHUR did keep the sword Excalibur throughout his life, but the sheath of the blade he did lose, and that through the treachery of one who should have been his dearest friend. And in the end, with the loss of that miraculous sheath, Arthur did suffer great pain and sorrow. And this is how this sorry happening came to pass.

After King Arthur, as aforesaid, had been victorious in two great battles, and after he had broken the power of King Lot and King Urien and those other kings who had opposed him, there fell upon the land a long and lasting peace. And by his noble virtues and high chivalry, the King did insure that tranquillity would reign. For indeed, King Arthur dispensed justice and mercy unto all his subjects, whether of high birth or of low.

Wherefore it came to pass, as it hath been told and illustrated with respect to the Sable Knight, that they who had been his enemies grew to love him and to faithfully serve him. And few held out against him.

But one whose hatred was deep and abiding was Queen Morgana le Fay, the King's own sister. And verily, Morgana was a sorceress.

Now this woman was a cunning enchantress, and mistress of so much magic that she could, by means of spells, work her will upon all things whether alive or dead, for verily Merlin himself had been her teacher in times past.

And Queen Morgana le Fay was wife unto that puissant lord King Urien of Gore, and she was mother unto that renowned knight Sir Ewaine, and she was, as aforesaid, half-sister unto King Arthur because the Lady Igraine was mother to both. And notwithstanding the honor accorded her and her exalted estate, ambition and hatred raged deep in the heart of her. Fain would she be queen of all the realm and not of Gore alone, and she bethought to herself that should Arthur die, then of a surety her husband, King Urien, would be proclaimed overlord of the realm. Thus would her own power be extended. Wherefore she did brood continually upon this matter, and the longer she thought upon it, the greater grew her hatred of Arthur.

Now Queen Morgana dwelt on the island of Avalon. And Avalon was verily a wondrously strange land, the like of which was not anywhere else in all the world. For this isle was like unto a paradise for beauty, being all covered with gardens of flowers, intermingled with plantations of fair trees, some bearing fruit and others all a-blossom. And many fair terraces of lawns lay all about the borders of the island. And in the midst of these fair gardens and orchards there rose a multitude of castles and towers, built the one above the other. And some of these castles were white as snow and some were gay with a multitude of colors.

But the greatest marvel of Avalon was this: that in the midst of those castles and towers was one single tower built entirely of loadstone. And in that tower lay the greatest mystery of the place, which mystery was controlled by the sorceress Morgana le Fay. For the island floated upon the surface of the water, and that tower of loadstone had a power so that, by its means, Avalon would float from place to place according to the will of Morgana le Fay. And betimes the isle of Avalon would be here, and betimes the isle of Avalon would be there, wheresoever that puissant enchantress willed it.

Wherefore only few people there were who had seen that island, for no one ever drew nigh to Avalon save by the authority of Queen Morgana le Fay. And at her bidding, the isle would be all covered o'er with a mist like unto a silver cloud. Then no mortal eye could behold Avalon. But betimes gay voices and sweet music would arise from its lawns and plantations, clear and thin because of the great distance, and he who listened from the shore would feel his soul grow faint, so sweet was the music from that enchanted isle. Then should the listener still muster strength to look out over the waters, then he might gaze on Avalon. Then would that island suddenly disappear, leaving him who had seen it to know that ne'er would he ever see its like again.

A Trust Betrayed

NOW SO POSSESSED was Morgana le Fay with her desire to be Queen of the realm that she plotted the destruction of King Arthur. Wherefore to this end she betook herself from the enchanted isle of Avalon and went to dwell at Camelot where the King held court.

Now after Queen Morgana le Fay had come to Camelot, she did comport herself like a devoted and loving sister, so that neither her brother nor even her husband did suspect that treachery which did lie in her heart. So it came to pass that one day as Queen Morgana and King Arthur did engage in friendly talk, Morgana expressed her desire to see that noble weapon Excalibur, and Arthur, proud of that mighty weapon, did promise he would show it to her. And, indeed, the next day he did summon Morgana, saying, "Sister, come with me, and I will show thee Excalibur."

Therewith did he take Morgana by the hand, and he led her into that room where she beheld a strong wooden coffer bound stoutly with bands of iron and studded all over with iron nails and fastened with three great locks. Then did the King unlock the coffer and he did lift the lid thereof. And there, encased in his magic sheath, lay the sword Excalibur. And King Arthur did say unto his sister, "Lady, take this sword and examine it as you please."

Therewith did Queen Morgana lift Excalibur out of the coffer, and she drew him out of his sheath and, lo! the blade flashed like lightning. Then she said, "Brother, I would fain take this mighty sword and would keep it with me yet a little while to enjoy this sight in full measure."

And so greatly did Arthur desire to show his sister his love for her that he said, "Lady, take thou Excalibur and his sheath." And she bore them away with her to her chambers.

Then straightaway did Queen Morgana send for sundry goldsmiths, eight in number, and for armorsmiths, eight in number, and for jewelers, eight in number, and she said unto them, "Make for me a sword that shall be in every particular like unto this sword that I have here." Thereupon she disclosed to them Excalibur in his sheath. So these eight goldsmiths and these eight armorsmiths and these eight lapidaries did labor with great diligence. And in a fortnight, they brought forth a sword so much like Excalibur that no mortal eye could determine which was the true sword and which was the false. And Queen Morgana le Fay kept both those swords beside her until her purposes should be ready for fulfillment.

A Gift of a Horse

A FEW DAYS afterward, Arthur did proclaim that a hunt would be held seven days hence. And on the day before this hunt, Morgana le Fay came unto King Arthur and she said, "Brother, I have brought thee a gift of love." Therewith she called out, and two grooms came forth leading a noble horse with a hide as black as jet and with trappings and harness all of shining silver. And that horse was so proud in its carriage and so exceedingly beautiful withal, that neither the King nor any other in that court had ever seen its peer.

And the King was filled with delight, and said, "Sister, verily this is the noblest gift that e'er did anyone give unto me."

"Ha! brother," quoth Queen Morgana, "I would that thou mightst consider that horse as a token of the devotion betwixt thee and me. And I beg thee that thou thyself wilt ride forth upon that horse at the hunt tomorrow day."

And King Arthur replied, "Happily will I do so." So the next day, according to his promise, he rode forth to the hunt upon that jet-black steed.

Now in the course of the hunt, the hounds discov-

ered a hart of great size, and with much eagerness did
the King and all of his court give chase. Now the magnificent black steed of King Arthur soon outstripped
the mounts of all the others, saving only that of a certain very honorable knight called Sir Accalon of Gaul.
Then did Sir Accalon and the King ride together at a
great pace through the forest, and so eager were they
with the chase that they knew not whither they rode.
When after long riding they did overtake the hart,
they found it embushed in a tangle of brushwood, and
there did Arthur slay that stag. Thus was the chase
ended.

Now the King and Sir Accalon set out to retrace
their way home, but ere they had ridden a mile or less
they did discover that the woodland was like unto a
maze and that they were lost therein. For so far had
they followed the chase that they had come to a country altogether strange. And they did wander hither and
thither until eventide, until they were sore oppressed
with hunger and with weariness. Then said King
Arthur to Sir Accalon, "Messire, meseems we shall
have nowhere to rest ourselves tonight except it be
beneath a tree within this forest."

Unto this Sir Accalon replied, "My lord, let us
permit our horses to seek their way through this wil-
derness. Haply they will bring us to some place of
habitation.

Now this advice appeared to King Arthur to be

sound, wherefore he set loose his bridle-rein and allowed the black horse to choose his own way. And Sir Accalon upon his steed followed fast after the King. In this manner did they travel a great distance into the forest, and the night did fall about them.

But before it grew entirely dark, they emerged from out that forest and, lo! they found themselves upon an open place whence they beheld a wide inlet of the sea. And before them was a beach of sand, wonderfully smooth and white. And they went down to that beach, and they knew not what to do, for no habitation did they see on any side.

Now while they stood filled with doubt before that harbor, they did perceive at a great distance a sailing ship which sped across the waters more speedily than any ship that these two had ever seen. And the ship was wonderful to behold, for it was painted all about in different colors, each more gaudy and more brilliant than the other, and the sails were all of silk.

Now as they stood upon the sand, the ship did draw nigh unto the harbor. And when the ship was landed, King Arthur said to Accalon, "Sir, let us walk forward and look upon this ship, for ne'er did I see her like before."

So did the twain walk down to where the ship lay. And as they gazed upon that ship and wondered what power had brought her thither, of a sudden they beheld a curtain part asunder. Then there issued forth from behind that curtain twelve beauteous damsels, clad in scarlet satin. Upon the head of each damsel did sit a circlet of gold, and round about her arms were bracelets of beaten gold.

Then came the twelve damsels forward, and they said, "Welcome, King Arthur! Welcome, Sir Accalon!"

At this, Arthur was deeply astonished, and he said, "Fair ladies, how is this? Ye appear to know me well, but I know ye not."

Unto this, the chiefest of those damsels made reply, "Sir, know ye that we are part fay. Therefore we know how ye have followed a long chase, and we know that ye are weary and that ye are hungered and athirst. Now within this ship ye may rest and refresh yourselves, and it would please us if ye would come aboard."

Now this did seem a kind and generous offering, wherefore King Arthur said to Sir Accalon, "Messire, I have great mind to follow out this adventure." Then the King said to the damsels, "Our need is sore, and ye are gracious to offer us succor."

Whereupon those ladies let fall a gangplank, and King Arthur and Sir Accalon spurred their horses aboard the ship. And no sooner had they come to the deck than the gangplank was lifted and the ship withdrew from the sands, and it sailed away as speedily as it had come. And no man trimmed the sails of that ship nor did anyone lay hand upon the rudder. Wherefore

King Arthur knew that that ship was a faerie vessel

Then did those twelve damsels aid King Arthur and Sir Accalon to dismount, and some led off their horses and others brought the knights to a fair chamber at the stern of the ship. And in this chamber was a table spread with cloth of fine linen and laden with savory meats and with the freshest of white breads and with wines, both red and white. And at the sight of this bountiful table, King Arthur and Sir Accalon rejoiced mightily, and gladly did they sit and dine.

Now when he had eaten his fill, a great drowsiness fell upon the King, and he said, "Fair damsels, my companion and I are grateful to ye beyond measure that ye have so kindly refreshed us, but I would now that ye had a place wherein we might sleep."

Unto this, the chiefest of the damsels did reply, "My lord, this boat was designed for your refreshment, wherefore have all things been made ready for ye."

Then was King Arthur conducted forth to a sleeping-chamber which had been prepared for him, and other damsels led Sir Accalon forth into a like chamber. And King Arthur marveled at the comeliness of his chamber, for the bedstead was of beaten gold and the hangings on the walls were made of cloth of gold. Then he laid himself down with much comfort to his body, and straightway he fell into a deep and gentle sleep, and he had no dream of any sort.

The King Is Captive

NOW WHEN ARTHUR stirred from that deep slumber, at first he knew not whether he still slept or whether he was indeed awake. For, lo! he woke to find that he lay upon a pallet of stone in a dark and dismal chamber made of stone. And he perceived that this gloomy chamber was in truth an underground dungeon, and all about him he did hear the sound of voices raised in woeful complaint. Then quoth King Arthur in great puzzlement, "Where is that fine ship where last night I was succored, and what hath become of those twelve beautiful damsels and of Sir Accalon?"

Then, looking about him, he beheld all about him in that dungeon numerous captive knights in very sad estate, and he understood that from these knights had issued that woeful lament that he had heard.

Whereupon did King Arthur raise himself from where he lay and he looked upon all those knights, and he saw that all the two and twenty knights who were prisoners in that place were strangers unto him.

Then King Arthur said unto those knights, "Messires, I pray ye tell me who ye are and what is this dread place wherein I find myself?"

To which the chiefest of those captive knights made reply, "Sir, we are prisoners within this dungeon, even as ye are, and this dungeon is verily the nether part of this castle. And castle and dungeon twain belong to a certain knight known as Sir Domas le Noir, who is indeed Sir Domas the Black.

"And last night were ye brought hither by two men clad in black, and these two did lay ye upon yonder pallet, nor did ye waken. Wherefore I may believe that ye are in the same case as we, and that ye are made a prisoner unto Sir Domas le Noir."

Then did King Arthur ask who was this Sir Domas, and what manner of man was he.

"Now shall ye hear," said the captive knight, and therewith he commenced upon this story:

"I believe," said he, "that this Sir Domas is the falsest knight that liveth, for he is full of treason and he is altogether a coward and craven in his heart. Yet is he a man of high estate, nor doth any man in these domains wield more power.

"Now there are two brothers, and Sir Domas is the one and the other is called Sir Ontzlake, and Sir Domas is the elder and Sir Ontzlake the younger. When the father of these two knights was like to die, he did divide his estates in twain in equal parts, and he left the one son equal patrimony with the other. But now hath it come about that Sir Domas keepeth nearly all of those estates and that Sir Ontzlake keepeth only one

castle, and that one castle he holdeth only by force of
arms and by his own courage. For though Sir Domas
is naught but coward, yet hath he cunning beyond any
other man. Wherefore hath it come about that of that
patrimony, Sir Domas hath all of it and Sir Ontzlake
hath none of it, saving only that one castle and estate.

"Now another man would be well satisfied with this.
But than Sir Domas no man is more greedy, nor can he
find pleasure in life until he possesseth that one castle
and estate. But Sir Ontzlake is an excellent knight and
puissant of limb. Wherefore to gain that estate must
Sir Domas meet his brother as man to man in a contest
of arms, or else he cannot acquire that coveted castle.
But this combat doth he not dare, because he is altogether craven.

"For many a day hath Sir Domas been in search of
a knight to do battle against Sir Ontzlake in his behalf.
And all the knights that he can arrest, he bringeth to
this castle and he giveth them their choice, whether to
take up his cause against his brother or to remain in
this place as his prisoner and without ransom. So hath
he arrested all of us, and he hath made demand of each
to do battle in his behalf. But not one of us will take
up the cause of that evil knight, wherefore do we all
remain his prisoners."

"Ha!" quoth King Arthur, "this is indeed a sorrowful tale. Nevertheless, methinks that should Sir Domas
make appeal to me, I will take up his cause. For rather

would I do battle for a villain than remain a prisoner the whole of my life. For a man is not brother to the mole, and he belongeth in the sunlight howsoever hard his lot may be.

...numerous captive knights in very sad estate

"Yet should I take this battle upon me and should I succeed in it, then will I do with Sir Domas in some other manner, nor will he like it well how I do deal with him."

Now a little while after King Arthur had done speaking, the door of that prison-house was opened by the porter, and a fair young damsel did enter in. And this damsel said unto Arthur, "Sir, it grieveth me to see so noble a knight made prisoner here. Yet may ye get your freedom back again, if ye will undertake to defend the cause of the lord of this castle."

To this, King Arthur made reply, "Lady, your lord's cause pleaseth me but little. Nevertheless, I will consent to take up his cause. But one condition I do impose: that if by grace of Heaven I win his battle, then all these, my companions in this dungeon, shall be freed as well as I."

"Be it so," quoth the damsel, "for that condition will content the master of this castle."

Then King Arthur looked more closely at the maiden, and he said, "Damsel, meseems I know thy face, and that perchance I have seen thee before."

"Nay, sir," said she, "ye cannot have seen me, for ne'er have I been at any place but this, and I am the daughter of the lord of this castle."

But she spoke false, for she was in truth a damsel of Morgana le Fay, and she was one of those damsels who had beguiled King Arthur onto the ship the night before, and it was she who had delivered him into the hands of Sir Domas. And all these things had she done upon the command of Queen Morgana.

Then quoth the King, "Before I take up this battle, ye must carry a message for me unto the court of King Arthur, and that message must be delivered only into the hands of Queen Morgana le Fay, and ye must bring me surety that that queen has got that message."

And the damsel said, "It will be done."

Whereupon King Arthur wrote a letter to Queen Morgana le Fay asking that she send to him his sword Excalibur, and he sealed that letter and gave it to the damsel.

And when Queen Morgana received that letter she laughed and said, "My lord shall have a sword, and it shall please his eye as well as Excalibur." Therewith she sent him that other sword that had been made for her in imitation of Excalibur, but Excalibur she kept by her.

So Sir Domas sent word unto his brother Sir Ontzlake that he had got himself a champion through whom he would take the little portion of their patrimony that Sir Ontzlake still held. And Sir Ontzlake was taken with great trouble of spirit, for he had of late been sore wounded at a tourney and a spear had been thrust through both his thighs. Now was he abed with that wound, and he could not himself defend his estate. Nor had he anyone to take up his cause.

The Adventure of
Sir Accalon

NOW SHALL YE learn what befell Sir Accalon the morning after he went aboard the magic ship with King Arthur.

When that good knight awoke, it was with him as it had been with King Arthur, that at first he knew not whether he still slept and was dreaming, or whether he had waked. For, lo! he lay beside a basin of white marble that held a shining silver spout and from that spout gushed a freshet of clear water. And nearby he perceived a large pavilion of many-colored brilliant silks; and a fair meadow of rich green grass bordered on that pavilion.

Then did Sir Accalon rise and cross himself, saying, "God save King Arthur from any harm, for I do think those damsels upon that ship have wrought some evil magic upon us to separate us the one from the other."

Now as he made some noise in bestirring himself, there came forth from the pavilion a monstrous dwarf. And the head of that dwarf was as big as that of a full-grown man, yet he stood no higher than a dog, for his legs were wondrous tiny. And his face was hideous to look upon, for his eyes were nearly closed with squinting, and his nose was hooked like the talon of an eagle, and his teeth jutted from his mouth. Nevertheless he was richly dressed, and he saluted Sir Accalon with due civility. Whereupon Sir Accalon said to the dwarf, "Sirrah, who are you?"

And the dwarf made answer, "Messire, I belong to the lady of yonder silk pavilion, Lady Gomyne of the Fair Hair. My lady hath bid me welcome ye to this place, and she would have ye dine with her."

"Ha! and prithee tell me how it was I came hither," said Sir Accalon.

"Sir," replied the dwarf, "that I do not know, for when we looked forth this morning we saw ye lying here alone by the fountain, but we did not see how came ye there."

And Sir Accalon did marvel at this. Then he knelt before the fountain and bathed himself, and then with the dwarf he went to the pavilion. And when he had come there, he found a table of silver spread with a fair white cloth and covered with abundant food and drink.

Now as soon as Sir Accalon was come into the pavilion, the curtains parted upon the further side, and there entered from another chamber a proud and beautiful lady, and she gave Sir Accalon welcome to that place. And Accalon said to her, "Lady, methinks ye are very civil."

"Nay, sir," said the lady. "Ye are not to thank me,

for I cannot help but be civil unto a knight as worthy as ye." And then quoth she, "Sir, will ye sit here at my table and break your fast with me?"

At this Sir Accalon was right glad, for he had not eaten that day. And furthermore, the beauty of that lady did please him exceedingly, so that he was greatly joyed to be in her company. So they two sat at table in pleasant spirit, and the dwarf waited upon them.

Then spoke the Lady of the Pavilion in this way, "Sir Knight, ye look a very strong and worthy lord and one well used to feats of arms."

And Sir Accalon made reply, "Lady, it beseemeth me not to speak of mine own worth, but this much I may freely say: that my friends and mine enemies both report that in knightly combat I do always conduct myself well."

Then the lady said, "I believe ye are a worthy knight. Wherefore might ye be of service to such another worthy knight as yourself, and one who is in sad need of knightly service."

To this Sir Accalon said, "Who is this knight and what is that service to be rendered him? And who are ye to him, that ye think so kindly of him?"

And the lady gave answer, "The name of that lord is Sir Ontzlake, and I am the lady of that lord." And this was that same Sir Ontzlake that was brother to Sir Domas le Noir. And the lady told Sir Accalon, even as aforesaid, how Sir Domas had deprived his brother of all of his patrimony, saving only one castle and one small estate. And she told how Sir Domas had found himself a champion to seize even that one little holding, and how Sir Ontzlake was grievously wounded, nor could he rise up from his bed and do battle, nor had he any champion to take his part.

"Wherefore," said that lady, "meseems a knight could have no better cause for which to show his prowess than in being that knight's champion."

And Sir Accalon made reply, "Lady, right willing would I be to defend Sir Ontzlake but, alas! I have neither arms nor armor with which to do battle."

Then that lady smiled with pleasure, and she said, "Messire, Sir Ontzlake hath armor that shall be altogether to your liking, and he would gladly give it ye. As for arms, I have here a sword that hath but one fellow in all the world."

Upon this, she went back into that curtained recess whence she had come, and when she came forth again, she carried in her hands a scarlet cloth. And she opened the cloth before Sir Accalon and, lo! within that cloth was the sword Excalibur in his sheath.

Then the lady said, "This sword shall be yours if ye will assume this quarrel upon behalf of Sir Ontzlake."

Now when Sir Accalon beheld that sword, he said in amazement, "Certes, either this is Excalibur, or else it is his twin." Therewith he drew the blade from out its sheath and it did shine with extraordinary splendor.

And Accalon said to the lady, "I am all filled with wonder. For this sword is indeed the very image of another sword I know of, but that sword belongeth to another."

And the lady smiled on him again, and said, "I have heard tell that in the world there is another sword like unto this."

Then did Sir Accalon exclaim, "Lady, to win this sword for myself I would gladly fight in any battle whatsoever."

And thus it came about that King Arthur did do battle unknowingly with a knight that he loved well. And that knight had Excalibur to use against his master. And all this came to pass through the wiles of the sorceress Morgana le Fay.

The Death of
a Valiant Knight

NOW FOR THAT battle a fair field was prepared, and thither came Sir Domas and Sir Ontzlake on the day assigned, each with his knight-champion and his attendants, and Sir Ontzlake was carried forth upon a litter because of the sore wound in his thighs. And a great many folk came to behold the combat, for news of it had gone forth about that place.

So at noon the two champions rode forth into the barriers of combat, and King Arthur was clad all in the armor of Sir Domas, and Sir Accalon was clad all in the armor of Sir Ontzlake, and the face of each was covered by his helmet. Wherefore neither of those two knew the other.

Then the herald took up his horn and blew upon it, and each knight put himself in readiness for the assault. Whereupon the herald did cry, "Charge!" and the two horses sprang forward with such speed and fury as was wonderful to behold, and their hoofbeats were as thunder to the ear. Then did King Arthur and Sir Accalon meet upon the course, and the spear of each knight burst into pieces, leaving only the truncheon which he held in his hand. Upon this, each knight voided his horse with great skill and threw aside the truncheon of his spear and straightway drew his sword.

At first they lunged, and then they struck and, lo! the sword of King Arthur did not bite into the armor of Sir Accalon, but the sword of Sir Accalon bit deeply into the armor of King Arthur, and so sorely was King Arthur wounded that the blood ran down in great quantities. And they struck again and yet again, very often and very powerfully, and as it was at first, so it was afterward: the sword of Sir Accalon ever bit into the armor of King Arthur, and the sword of King Arthur bit not at all into his enemy's armor. And the armor of Arthur was stained all over with the red blood, and the grass at their feet was covered with the blood of that good King. But Sir Accalon bled not at all because he wore the sheath of Excalibur at his side.

Now when King Arthur saw how all the ground was wet with his own blood and how his enemy bled not at all, he began to fear that he would die in that battle. Wherefore he said to himself, "How is this? Hath the virtue departed out of Excalibur and his sheath? Almost might it be that the sword that cutteth me so sorely is Excalibur and the sword that I hold is some other sword."

Then a great despair of death came upon King Arthur and he ran at Sir Accalon and smote him so fierce a blow upon the helm that Sir Accalon fell down upon the ground. But at that blow, the sword of King

Arthur broke off at the cross of the handle, and the pommel and the cross were all that the King still held in his hand.

Now at that blow Sir Accalon waxed exceedingly wroth, and he ran at King Arthur, meaning to strike him such a blow as would end that battle. But when he saw what state his enemy was in, he paused in his assault and said, "Sir Knight, ye have no weapon and ye have lost much blood. Wherefore I demand ye to yield yourself unto me."

Then again was King Arthur very much in dread that his death was near. But he was the King; therefore he might not yield to any knight. Whereupon he said, "Nay, Sir Knight, sooner would I die with honor than yield and lose mine honor. Since I have no weapon, ye may slay me if ye will. But I warn ye that slaying will be to your shame and not to my shame, as ye will learn betimes."

"As ye will it," said Sir Accalon. "I will not spare ye if ye will not yield." Whereupon Sir Accalon smote him such a woeful blow that the King fell down upon his knees. Then Sir Accalon raised Excalibur to strike again, whilst all the people who were there cried out to him to spare so worshipful a knight.

Now at that trial-at-arms was present a certain damsel of surpassing beauty named Vivien, and this damsel had learned magic from the enchanter Merlin and Merlin had disclosed to her divers secrets of sorcery.

Wherefore though she was but fifteen years of age this Vivien was passing wise and powerful. Now as she beheld that dolorous assault Vivien did take counsel and she said, "Certes, that is a right valiant knight who is so near death. Methinks he ought not die, seeing how he hath fought so bravely."

So when Sir Accalon raised his sword a second time, Vivien did clap her hands loudly, and she uttered a spell so potent that a great cloud rushed across the sun, and the sky grew dusky. And it seemed to Sir Accalon that he had been struck a powerful blow upon his arm, for verily his arm was benumbed all from the finger-tips unto the hollow of his armpit. And Excalibur fell out of his hands and onto the grass.

Now when King Arthur came close up to that sword, he perceived at once that it was Excalibur, wherefore he knew he had been betrayed. So he cried out thrice in a loud voice, "Treason! Treason! Treason!" And as he cried aloud, the dark cloud passed and the sun shone bright upon the land. Then King Arthur set his knees upon the blade, and before Sir Accalon could stay him, he seized that sword into his hands.

And when he took up that sword, a great strength came into King Arthur, and he arose from his knees and ran at Sir Accalon, and he smote him so sorely that the blade penetrated his armor. But, lo! no blood rushed from the wound, though it was deep to the depth of half a palm's breadth. And King Arthur

smote again and again and Sir Accalon cried out, and
he fell down upon his hands and knees. Then King
Arthur caught up the sheath of Excalibur, and he
plucked it away from Sir Accalon and flung it to the
ground. And now the wounds of Sir Accalon burst
out bleeding in great measure. And King Arthur
snatched off the helmet of Accalon, for indeed he
meant to slay him.

Now because King Arthur was blinded with his
own blood, he did not know Sir Accalon, and he said,
"Sir Knight, who art thou who hast betrayed me?"

And Sir Accalon said, "Who are ye to say I have be-

"Treason! Treason! Treason!"

trayed ye? I am no traitor. Rather am I Sir Accalon of Gaul and I am knight in good worship of King Arthur's court."

Now when King Arthur heard this, he exclaimed in a loud voice, "How is this? Dost not know who I am?"

"Nay, I know you not," Sir Accalon replied.

"I am thy master," the King said, and he took off his helmet.

And when Sir Accalon beheld King Arthur he swooned away and lay like one dead upon the ground. And King Arthur said, "Take him hence."

And when the people saw what knight had been champion for Sir Domas, they burst over the barriers and they ran toward the King. But as they came nigh him, Arthur swooned away because of the great measure of blood he had lost. Wherefore all those people took great sorrow, thinking the King must die, and they bemoaned themselves without stint.

Then came the fair maid Vivien out into that field and she said, "Give him up to me, and I will heal him." Then did she call for two litters, and in one she placed King Arthur, and she placed Sir Accalon in the other. And both knights bore she away to a priory of nuns that was nearby.

Then did Vivien uncover the wounds of the King and did bathe them with a precious balsam, and immediately those wounds began to heal.

And by the next morning, King Arthur was much

recovered. Though he was yet exceeding weak, he rose up from his couch, and he wrapped a cloak about him and went to the chamber where Sir Accalon lay. There he bid Sir Accalon to recount his adventures. And when Sir Accalon told how the lady of Sir Ontzlake had given him a sword wherewith to battle, King Arthur did question that knight carefully.

And the King perceived that that lady was in no wise loyal to Sir Ontzlake but that she was a sorceress. Whereupon he said, "Messire, thou art not to be blamed in this matter. But I do fear that there is treachery here to encompass my ruin."

Then he went out from that chamber and he found Vivien and he did say, "Gentle damsel, I beseech thee to dress the wounds of that knight with that same balsam thou didst use to dress my wounds."

"Lord," said Vivien, "I cannot do so, for I have no more of that balsam." But what she said was false, for she did have more of that balsam, but she did not choose to use it upon Sir Accalon. And Sir Accalon died before nightfall of the wounds he had received in battle against King Arthur.

Now ye may wonder that Vivien did heretofore work a potent spell to succor King Arthur in battle, yet for his companion she would not spare a little balsam though she had it ready at hand. And the reason is this: that Vivien was part fay and she hated all mortal men, but her master, Merlin, had set a spell upon her so that she must in all ways serve King Arthur. But Merlin had set no spell concerning Sir Accalon, wherefore she let that good knight die.

Now in the afternoon of that same day King Arthur did summon Sir Domas and Sir Ontzlake. And so awesome was his look that when the twain came before him, those two knights could not stand upright, but fell down upon their knees.

Then quoth the King, "Do thou rise, Sir Ontzlake, and I will pardon thee, for thou knewest not what thou didst. But thou, Sir Domas, art a false and treasonable knight, wherefore I do deprive thee of all thy possessions. Thou shalt have only that single castle that thy brother had. But all the holdings that heretofore were thine, those do I give unto Sir Ontzlake. And I further ordain that thou shalt nevermore ride upon any horse save a palfrey, a horse fitting only for women, for thou art not worthy to ride upon a courser like a true knight. And I command it of thee, that when thou hast liberated as thou hast promised all those knights who were my companions in captivity, then thou shalt likewise recompense them for all the injury thou hast done unto them, according as it shall be decided by a court of chivalry."

Therewith he dismissed those two knights and they verily rejoiced that he had dealt with them so mercifully.

The Treachery of Morgana

NOW WHEN THE news of that combat was brought to Queen Morgana le Fay and she learned that Sir Accalon was dead, she could not surmise wherein her designs had miscarried. Also did she wonder how much King Arthur had divined of her treachery. So she did take counsel, saying, "I will go to my brother, and will learn what I may. If he knoweth of my treason, I will beseech him to pardon my transgression." Then she gathered together her court of knights and esquires, and she went thither to that priory where King Arthur did abide.

And when she had come to his chamber, she asked of his attendants what cheer had the King. And they made answer, "He is asleep and he must not be wakened."

But Morgana replied, "I am not to be forbidden, for I must speak with him." And they did not dare to stay her because she was the King's sister.

So Morgana le Fay passed lightly into the chamber where the King lay and he did not waken at her coming. So she plotted and said, "I will take Excalibur and his sheath, and I will carry them away with me to

Avalon and never again shall my brother behold them." Then she went quietly to where the King lay, and she looked upon him as he slept, and she did perceive that Arthur had Excalibur beside him and that he held the pommel of the sword in his hand, even while he slept. Then Morgana thought, "Alas for this! If I try to take Excalibur, my brother will awaken and verily will he slay me for my treason."

Now the sheath of Excalibur lay at the foot of the couch. So softly did she take up that sheath, and she did wrap it in her mantle, and she did go out of that

chamber. And King Arthur did not awaken at her going. And Morgana le Fay said to the King's attendants, "Do not waken my brother, for he sleepeth soundly." Therewith she mounted her horse and went her way from that place.

Now when King Arthur awoke, he perceived that the sheath of Excalibur was gone, and he said in anger, "Who hath been here?"

And they in attendance made answer, "Queen Morgana le Fay hath been here. She came in and did see

...she pitched it out into the water.

that ye were sleeping, and she did go her way without waking ye."

Then of a sudden did King Arthur perceive all the woeful events that had befallen him, and he said, "I fear that she hath dealt treacherously with me from the beginning to the end of these adventures."

Whereupon he arose and summoned all his knights and esquires to pursue Morgana, although he was still passing faint from his sore wounds and from his loss of blood.

Seeing him, the party of Queen Morgana spurred their horses the faster, until they came to a hill where no trees grew. And at the crest of that hill was a vast lake. Then did Morgana le Fay take the sheath of Excalibur in both her hands, and she swung it by its belt above her head, and she pitched it out into the water a great distance.

Now King Arthur had just come to the foot of the hill, and he saw what his sister did upon the crest of that hill, and he grieved heavily.

And, lo! there suddenly appeared out of the water a woman's arm, clad in white samite and adorned with many bracelets. And the hand of that arm caught the sheath of Excalibur and drew it underneath the water. And no eye ever again beheld that magic sheath.

So by an act of foul treachery was the sheath of Excalibur lost. And in time to come, that happening would verily prove a grievous thing for Arthur.

A King Disguised

NOW KING ARTHUR had reigned six months upon the throne and he had so pacified the realm that all but a few petty kingdoms were pledged unto him. Wherefore if one sought to display valor and prowess at arms he would come to Camelot; and the greatest knights in Britain did repair unto that court to serve King Arthur. And King Arthur was barely nineteen years of age.

Now when King Arthur had come onto the throne, the most part of the kings of his realm did gladly acknowledge him rightwise King over all. And yet other kings acknowledged him as their liege lord after defeat in battle. But there remained some few enemies of the realm.

And one of these enemies was King Ryence of North Wales. By nature was he ill-tempered and evil, and continually did he make a mock of King Arthur. And another enemy was Duke Mordaunt of North Umber, a cousin to King Ryence. And Mordaunt was verily a mighty warrior, but more evil in aspect and more violent of temper than any other knight in Britain.

Upon a certain day in that first summer of his reign did Arthur proclaim a high feast. To this feast were bidden seven kings and five queens in royal state, three score and seven lords and ladies of degree, and a multitude of worthy knights; and the foremost of these knights were accounted as the most valiant knights in Christendom.

Now when King Arthur looked about him at that feast, he saw that of all this noble gathering of kings and lords and knights not one man looked askance at his neighbor, but all were united in peace and amity. Wherefore, remembering how aforetime there had been discord throughout the realm, the King bethought himself, "Certes, wondrous it is how this reign of mine hath knit men together in kindliness and good fellowship." Wherefore because of his pleasure in his noble court his spirit sang within him.

Yet ever and anon at that joyful feast a cloud would seem to pass over the King for a sudden he would grow strangely solemn. And the reason for this melancholy was that Arthur had had a vision, and the memory of that vision did keep with him by day and by night. Nor was it a vision of a heavenly thing nor of a fay, but of a mortal lady. Yet that lady was so surpassing beauteous she might for her loveliness have been an angel. And that lady was the gentle Guinevere, the daughter of King Leodegrance of Cameliard in the west-country. Many days past had she come upon Arthur when he lay close to his death from wounds inflicted by the Sable Knight, and at her command did a leech heal the King. And from that very hour was the heart of Arthur filled with love for her. Therefore was the Lady Guinevere continually in his thoughts. And indeed he did believe there was no lady in the realm he would take for wife, save that fair lady.

Yet always ere the melancholy grew too heavy upon him, the King would look up and bend his thoughts to the glad feast before him and to the good company of that noble assembly.

Now while the King sat at feast and was both gay and solemn, lo! there rode into Camelot a herald-messenger from King Leodegrance of the west-country.

And at once was King Arthur cheered, thinking he must get news of the Lady Guinevere. But, in truth, the herald did bear tidings far less happy.

And that herald knelt before the King and spoke in this wise: "My liege lord, when ye in your majesty brought peace to the greater part of this realm, ye did reduce the power of my master, King Leodegrance. And all those knights who once paid homage at the court of Leodegrance have since come hither, so that worthy monarch can scarce defend himself against the predators of his lands. And now my master hath found sore trouble. For his enemy—and thine enemy as well —King Ryence of North Wales doth threaten to bring war unto Cameliard. Wherefore my master doth beseech aid of ye who are his King and overlord."

Then did the countenance of King Arthur grow dark with anger against him who would despoil the peace of the realm. And he said to that herald, "Certes, by my love for thy lord, I will give him what aid I am able so soon as I know his cause is just. Therefore tell me, herald, for what reason doth King Ryence threaten battle?"

"King Ryence doth make two demands upon my master," quoth the herald-messenger. "The first is that King Leodegrance cede unto King Ryence those lands of Cameliard that touch upon the border of North Wales. And the second is that the Lady Guinevere, the daughter of King Leodegrance, be delivered in marriage unto the cousin of King Ryence, Duke Mordaunt of North Umber."

Now when King Arthur had heard these words he

was seized with a surpassing anger, and his eyes seemed to shoot forth sparks, and his face flamed like fire. Then he rose and went forth from the hall, and those who beheld his wrath shuddered and turned their eyes away from his countenance. Nor could they understand how such petty lords as Ryence and Mordaunt might move so great a lord to so much ire. For the knights of his court knew not of the love of Arthur for Guinevere.

Then the King did enter into an inner room of the castle. And all alone he strode to and fro for a great while and no one of his household did dare to come nigh.

And each time he thought of that wicked duke who did demand marriage with Guinevere, then was King Arthur seized with a rage so violent it shook his body like a mighty wind.

When he did becalm himself, the King summoned unto him Sir Kay and Sir Ulfius. And he bid Sir Ulfius and Sir Kay to gather together a large army and bring that army to the castle Tintagalon in Cameliard, near the border of North Wales.

And the next day did Arthur himself set forth for Tintagalon with Merlin and with four famous knights of his court, to wit: Sir Gawaine and Sir Ewaine (who were nephews unto the King), Sir Pellias, and Sir Geraint.

And those six traveled across the forest to the land of Cameliard, two days and a night, until they came to the great stone castle of Tintagalon. Here was Arthur received with great rejoicing, for wheresoever the King went, the people loved him dearly.

Now the morning after King Arthur and his party had come unto Tintagalon, the King bid Merlin to walk with him in the garden. And there in that garden did King Arthur open his heart, and he spoke of his love for the Lady Guinevere. And when he had told of his love, he said, "Now, by the rood, Merlin, I swear it, and by mine honor I swear it, no other man on this earth shall take that fair lady to wife. Therefore, Merlin, I would go into the court of Cameliard that I may look on her all at my leisure. Yet must I come as some other, lest if she know I am the King, she honor me for my high estate and not for any worth of mine."

Now Merlin was cunning in magic and he did readily agree to aid Arthur, saying, "I will give thee such disguise that none in all the world shall know who thou art."

And within the hour, Merlin did convey unto the King a little cap. And when Arthur set that magical cap upon his head, he did appear like a rude rustic, a country bumpkin of little worth. And when he removed that cap, he became once again the noble king he in truth was. And it was as if he were the sun and that cap were a black cloud, for when that cap was on his head not one ray of his kingliness shone forth. But when he took it off, he verily seemed more noble than before.

And King Arthur said, "I will labor within the gardens of Cameliard. For the gardens will be the province of the mistress of that place; and as the wife of King Leodegrance is dead, the Lady Guinevere doth take her stead. Yea, it is in her gardens that I may readily see her and not be noticed by her withal.

"Yet haply sometime I may show her a little part of my true self, ere I court her for my Queen. For I would liefer she loved me for my knighthood than for my kingship, and I would have her honor me for mine own self and not because I am overlord of this realm."

Then did King Arthur cover his royal garments with a jerkin of rouge frieze, and that jerkin did even hide the golden collar he wore about his neck. And unknown to any man save Merlin, he did quit Tintagalon and took his way on foot to Cameliard.

Now the town of Cameliard was large and comely. And foremost of the buildings in that place was the great castle of King Leodegrance. And all round the towers of that castle were fair lawns and gardens and orchards of apple and cherry. And overhead among the turrets of that castle flew great flocks of pigeons. And it was dusk when Arthur came up to that castle. And the King was dressed in the guise of an humble peasant when he came unto Cameliard to meet his adventure.

Now when Arthur had got within the castle gates,

he did seek out the head-gardener and asked that worthy to be taken into the service of the Lady Guinevere. And the gardener looked upon him and saw that he was tall and strong, wherefore he thought the lad would serve his mistress altogether well. And thus did Arthur, overlord of all Britain, become a gardener's boy at Cameliard.

The Stranger Knight

NOW THE KING was altogether delighted to serve in the garden of Lady Guinevere. For in that pleasant summer season Guinevere did walk every day among the flowers with her maidens, and soon did Arthur perceive how gentle was that lady's nature. Thus passed seven days, nor did Arthur any whit lament that for such time he had enjoyed none of his kingly estate but fared no better than any gardener's boy.

Now on the morning of the eighth day, Lady Guinevere woke earlier than was her custom. So leaving her maidens still sleeping, she did open the casement of her chamber and she did look down into the rose-garden below. In that garden just beneath her window, there stood the marble figure of a youth holding a vase, and a fountain of clear water flowed out from that vase into a marble basin. And that figure and that fountain and that basin did all three lie in the shadow of a linden tree. And all around those three things stood a growth of roses, so thick that no eye might behold those three things, save from that one window.

Now as the Lady Guinevere gazed down out of that window, a knight came to that fountain ard knelt beside it and bathed his face in the clear waters. And the sunlight fell through the leaves of the linden tree and lay upon that knight. And Guinevere did perceive that his hair and his beard were the color of red gold, and that his brow and his throat were white as alabaster. And around his neck and his shoulders was there clasped a golden collar.

And he was indeed so graceful and so pleasing to behold withal that the Lady Guinevere did not know if this strange knight were a figure in a dream, or if he were a spirit, or if he were, in truth, a mortal man.

Wherefore as she did gaze down upon him she wondered mightily whether his face were as noble as his manner. For at all times was his face turned from her so that she could not see his visage. Therefore she turned and sped to the turret stairs and she did run down them and out into that garden. Likewise did she run through that garden in all silence until she came to the path that led to that marble fountain.

But for all her quietness, the King—for verily it was he—did hear her coming. Whereupon he set the magic cap again upon his head, and when Guinevere drew near she found no one by the fountain save the gardener's boy. And she said unto him, "Prithee, who was that strange knight who was here beside this fountain, and whither hath he taken himself?"

And the gardener's boy did reply, "Lady, there hath been no one here but me."

"Nay, fellow," she said, "thou dost deceive me. For with mine own eyes did I behold a young knight bathe himself in the fountain."

And the gardener's boy said once again, "Lady, there hath been no one here but me."

At this, Guinevere did gaze upon the gardener's boy in great perplexity, nor could she disbelieve him, seeing there was no reason wherefore he should lie to her. But neither might she believe him. Therefore she knew not what to think, and because of her perplexity, that lady was greatly displeased with him. "Truly, lad," quoth she, "if thou dost deceive me, thou shalt rue it." And thereupon in all wonderment she left that garden.

And all that day as Lady Guinevere sat over her embroidery, she did not cease to wonder how that strange knight had so suddenly vanished, and how the gardener's boy had come to be there in his stead. But as the sun began to set, she did bethink herself and she did call unto her maiden, Mellicene of the White Hand, saying, "Go and tell the gardener's lad to fetch unto me a basket of fresh roses wherewith to adorn my chamber."

Now when the gardener's lad came into that chamber, he held a great basket of roses. But, lo! he wore his cap upon his head. Therefore Mellicene of the White Hand did say unto him, "How now, Sir Rudeness! Dost thou know so little of what is due unto a princess that thou dost wear thy cap in the presence of

Guinevere did not know if this strange knight were a
figure in a dream

the Lady Guinevere? Now I bid thee straightway to
take thy cap from off thy head."

Whereupon the gardener's boy replied, "Lady, I
cannot take off my cap, for it will not be seemly, seeing I have an ugly place on my head."

"Then, boy, wear thy cap," said Lady Guinevere,
laughing, "only carry thou the roses unto me."

But when he had come nigh unto her, Guinevere received the flowers with her right hand, and with her left did she snatch the lad's cap and did pluck it from off his head. Whereupon in the instant was the gardener's boy transformed, and he stood before her as noble a young knight as ever was, with hair and beard like gold.

And Guinevere was so amazed she let fall the basket, and the roses lay all scattered at her feet. Now some of those ladies-in-waiting shrieked, and verily some were speechless from amazement. But not one of them knew that proud knight to be King Arthur.

Only the Lady Guinevere did perceive that this was that knight whom she had encountered in the cell of the forest hermit. But she had not learned the name of that knight, nor did she now learn it.

Then Guinevere laughed and flung his cap to him, saying, "Take thy cap and go thy ways, thou gardener's boy who hath an ugly place on his head."

But Arthur did not make reply to her words nor to her laughter, and most soberly did he set the magic cap back upon his head. Then did he turn and quit that room, leaving the roses scattered over the floor of that chamber just as they had fallen.

Now after that day whenever the Lady Guinevere would come upon the gardener's lad, she would say aloud to her maidens in a manner that Arthur might hear, "Lo! yonder is the gardener's lad who hath an ugly place upon his head, and always must he wear his cap to hide so unseemly a blemish."

Thus did she mock him, but in her chamber she bade her maidens to say naught, but to keep unto themselves this strange adventure. And Arthur, though he feigned not to hear her, was well pleased to know that his true-love was so spirited a lady.

A Challenge and a Champion

NOW THE NEXT morning there came a messenger unto the court at Cameliard with news that King Ryence of North Wales and his cousin, Duke Mordaunt of North Umber, were approaching, and that they did bring with them a numerous court of high-born knights and ladies. And King Leodegrance was greatly troubled in spirit.

And when in the early afternoon of that day King Ryence and Duke Mordaunt did appear before the castle, Leodegrance did go forth to greet them and they three met together at the castle gates. And there did King Leodegrance bid them welcome and did invite them into the castle where he might entertain them according to their degree.

But to this courtesy King Ryence deigned no pleasing reply, saying, "Nay, we go not with ye until we learn if ye are our friend or our foe. Wherefore we ask, will ye satisfy our demands? To wit, that to me ye give those lands that I lay claim to, and to my cousin, Duke Mordaunt, ye give the Lady Guinevere for wife.

"For five days will we abide outside your castle. And if ye meet our demands, then we are friends. But if ye do otherwise, then are we enemies come to wage war."

Then quoth Duke Mordaunt, "Sir King, I am in readiness to contest your daughter's hand with any knight of your court who hath a mind to deny me. Let him who is your champion step forth to assay a bout of arms with me, if he will."

Then was King Leodegrance downcast in spirit for he feared those proud lords, and he did return to his castle in melancholy mien.

But King Ryence and Duke Mordaunt and all their hosts did set up their pavilions, and the meadow was entirely covered with their habitations. And they took up with great feasting and merry-making.

Now the next morning Duke Mordaunt of North Umber did ride forth clad all in shining armor. And he rode to and fro before that castle and sent a saucy challenge to those within, daring any knight to come forth and encounter him. "Ho!" he cried, "how now, ye knights of Cameliard! Is there no one to come forth? Hath not Leodegrance even one champion?"

But none dared come forward, for Duke Mordaunt was accounted as one of the most puissant knights of that day. And all knew that there was no knight amongst the followers of King Leodegrance who was in any manner the equal of that skilled and haughty warrior.

Therefore did those lords and ladies that looked down upon him from the walls of Cameliard grieve, and they were ashamed. But all the lords and knights of the court of King Ryence did laugh and jeer and clap their hands, and they did cheer Duke Mordaunt as he rode up and down before them. And the more mirthful were they, the more abashed was the court of Cameliard.

Now all this while Arthur dug in the garden, until no longer could he abide the shame of Leodegrance. Wherefore he lay aside his spade and departed the castle secretly and went up into the town.

Now there dwelt in the town of Cameliard a merchant of exceeding wealth, by name Ralph of Cardiff. So manifold were his possessions and so rich his estate that his wealth was talked about in all parts of the realm. Accordingly it was to his house that the King directed his steps.

And before he entered the merchant's house, Arthur did remove his magic cap and once again assumed his kingly appearance. Wherefore the merchant was greatly surprised that so noble a lord should come before him clad only in frieze.

"Good Ralph of Cardiff," quoth King Arthur, "ye surely know how the Duke of North Umber doth ride up and down before the castle of Cameliard and doth send a scoffing challenge to those within to meet him in single combat in behalf of the King's daughter. Wherefore am I of a mind to assay that combat, that the honor of Cameliard may be upheld and that shame may be brought down upon her enemies.

"Now I have with me naught but this frieze jerkin, but ye have in your treasury suits of armor wrought so excellent that their fame hath reached even my ears though I dwell a great distance from this place. Wherefore I beseech ye to accouter me that I may straightway encounter yonder boastful knight.

"And, that ye may know that I crave armor for no other purpose save honorable combat, I will tell ye that I am verily a knight in disguise, a true friend to King Leodegrance who doth wish him well."

Whereupon did Arthur open the breast of his jerkin and he did show the merchant the gold collar about his neck. And then he showed that good man his signet ring, and when the merchant saw it, he did know it for the ring of the overlord of Britain. Wherefore he knew this was a knight of the court of King Arthur, and he did arise in honor to the stranger knight.

"My lord," quoth Master Ralph, "I perceive that ye are no ordinary errant knight. Wherefore it doth please me greatly to give ye whatsoever ye ask. But were ye not who ye are, and were ye indeed some lesser knight —nay, were ye naught but a peasant—yet would I be altogether willing to equip ye, seeing that ye ride forth against the hated Duke Mordaunt."

Then did Ralph of Cardiff ring a little silver bell. Whereupon several attendants came into that chamber.

And into their hands did that merchant entrust the person of the King and he bid his servants to do that knight full honor. Whereupon they prepared for Arthur a bath of warm water perfumed with ambergris. And after he was bathed, they did dry him with soft linen towels. Then they did conduct him to a hall all hung with tapestries and embroideries, where a feast was spread for his refreshment. And the lordly merchant himself did administer unto the King.

And afterwards six pages clad Arthur in Spanish armor, all cunningly wrought and all inlaid with gold. And the like of that armor was hardly to be found in all of Britain. For the doublet and the trappings of that armor were all of glistening satin and were as white as milk. And the shield was white and entirely without emblazonment or device of any sort.

And then did enter a seventh page, bearing a sword encrusted with jewels and wrought of a powerful alloy such that that sword was mightier than any sword save one—Excalibur that was at Camelot. And the page held the sword of Ralph of Cardiff in both his hands for it was passing heavy, but Arthur did take it up lightly in his one hand, and well pleased with it was he.

Then did those pages conduct the King into the courtyard where stood a noble war horse as white as milk, and all the trappings of that horse were of milk-white cloth, and also without emblazonment or adornment of any sort.

Now when the attendants had aided King Arthur to mount that lordly steed, Master Ralph did come forward and gave Arthur words of cheer. Then did he and the King bid adieu of one another, and King Arthur spurred his horse and rode away, all shining in white and glittering in fine armor. And King Arthur did resemble on that day the full moon in harvest season. And as he rode down the stony streets of Cameliard, all eyes did turn and gaze after him.

Now when Arthur did come unto the postern gate of the castle, he dismounted and he accosted an attendant, demanding speech with the Lady Guinevere. And the attendant, all amazed at that lordly stranger, did bring that message to Guinevere. Wherefore she came forth upon her gallery.

And when King Arthur looked up and saw her lovely visage, then was his heart filled again with love of her. And he said unto her, "Lady, I would fain do ye all honor that I am able. Therefore I now go forth to do combat with yonder duke, he who rideth up and down before this castle scoffing its tenants. Verily, I will assay his downfall. Wherefore I do beseech of ye some token such as a lady giveth a knight to wear when he doth ride forth to do her honor."

Then said the Lady Guinevere, "First must ye raise your visor, that I may look upon your face."

And King Arthur quoth, "Lady, this is not our hour. Haply ye shall know me by and by."

Then was the Lady Guinevere flattered and perplexed, but she quoth straightway, "I take ye gladly for my champion. And whatsoever token ye ask of me, that token will I give ye."

And the King replied, "Meseems that if I wore about my arm that necklace that ye now wear at your throat, my valor would be benefited."

"Sir Knight," said the Lady, "whatsoever ye ask of me, ye shall have." Thereupon she did unclasp the string of pearls, and she did drop it down from off her balustrade.

And the King caught the necklace and tied it about his arm. Whereupon he saluted that lady with knightly grace, and she did salute him.

Then straightway he went forth from that place, all filled with joy, for dearly did he love that lady.

A Famous Knight
Overthrown

NOW WHEN THE report had got about that a knight was come to do battle with the Duke of North Umber, there did gather on the walls of the castle a great crowd of courtiers, and on the walls of the town the common people were likewise all gathered. And so numerous and glad a concourse did assemble as would encourage any knight to do his utmost. And each man asked his neighbor who was this knight, and they made much talk and clamor above the battlefield.

Then at high noon, the herald did wind his horn and all that multitude did hush. Whereupon the portcullis of the castle was lifted and the narrow bridge was let fall, and forth did ride the White Champion. As he crossed that bridge, the hoofs of his war horse thundered on the boards, and when he came out into the sunlight, lo! his armor sparkled like lightning. And the people gave up a great cheer.

And when that cheer was stilled, Duke Mordaunt rode forward and he spoke a knightly greeting. "Messire," quoth he, "ye bear no crest upon your helm, nor have ye any device upon your shield, wherefore I know not who ye are. Nevertheless I know ye for a knight

of proven courage, or else ye would not have come
forth."

"Certes," said King Arthur, "my quality is the equal
of your own. And as for my courage, I have proved it
in as many encounters as ye have, and haply more."

"Ye speak with a large spirit," quoth the Duke. "Yet
ye would do better to make such prayers as ye are able,
for soon shall I cast ye down from your seat so that ye
will never rise again. For so have I served better men
than ye may ever hope to be." And they met in the
midst of the course and each brought his spear to the
other's shield, with a noise like thunder.

And, lo! the spear of the Duke of North Umber
burst into splinters, but the spear of the White Champion held fast. And the Duke was cast out of his saddle
like a windmill whirling in the air, and he did strike
the earth so heavily that the ground beneath him did
shudder. And thrice did he roll over ere he ceased to
fall.

Then all the people upon the walls shouted with
gladness, for they had not dared believe that their
champion would prove so strong and skillful. And
light of heart was Arthur, seeing the honor he had done
his chosen lady.

Whereupon esquires and men-at-arms of the court
of King Ryence did come running unto the fallen
knight, and they did unlace his helmet to give him air.
And at first they accounted him dead, for the Duke of

North Umber lay without life or motion. Nor did he recover from that swoon for the space of two hours.

Now when Arthur perceived that his enemy was not dead, he did turn his horse and rode off from Cameliard. For too blithe of spirit was he after that battle to return straightway to play again at being the humble gardener's boy.

And the Duke was cast out of his saddle

Wherefore he did choose to ride out beside the woodland, and for destination he did choose a certain grove that he had passed in his journey to the castle. For in that place woodchoppers were felling trees, and he thought to leave his horse and his armor in their care until he should once more have need of these accouterments.

My Lady's Servants

NOW THAT SUMMER'S day was sweet and pleasant, and sweet and pleasant were the thoughts of valiant King Arthur. And betimes he sang cheerily, and betimes he thought merrily upon his lady, and altogether he sat right gaily in his saddle as he did ride toward the grove of the woodchoppers.

Now in the distance he could see a tall and slender tower set upon a green hillock. And as he neared that tower, he perceived upon its balcony three fair damsels, clad all in green cloth. And on the high road at the foot of that tower, there sat a knight upon a horse, and that knight did play upon a lute and he sang sweetly to those three ladies on the balcony. And whene'er that knight would cease his singing, then those three ladies did clap their hands together and did bid him sing again. And gladly did he sing at their command.

All this King Arthur beheld, and the sight did please him. And as he drew nigh, lo! he perceived that he knew that knight. For though the knight was clad all in fine armor and his helmet did hide his face, yet did the King know the griffins engraved on his shield. And those griffins were the device of Sir Geraint, who

138

had accompanied him from Camelot to Tintagalon.

Now when Sir Geraint perceived a knight approaching, he ceased his singing and slung his lute behind him, and he turned to those ladies above him, saying, "Gentle ladies, ye have been pleased to listen to these songs that I have sung in your honor. Now likewise in your honor will I perform a deed of knightly prowess. For if ye will be so kind as to lend me your encouragement and not withdraw your beauty from this place, ye shall behold me overthrow yonder knight, and that to your honor."

Whereupon those ladies, flattered at Sir Geraint's words, paid him compliment on his noble bearing and address, and did wish him great success in the adventure he would undertake in their honor. Then did Sir Geraint straightway close the visor of his helmet, and dressing his spear and his shield, he went forth to meet Arthur.

Now Sir Geraint knew not the King, for verily the face of Arthur was covered with his helmet and he did wear no crest upon his helmet nor any device upon his shield.

"Ha! Messire," cried Sir Geraint, in high spirit. "I am minded to do ye honor, though I know not who ye are. For I will run a tilt with ye out of good fellowship and on behalf of the three fair damsels at yonder balcony. For I do affirm that those ladies are fairer than your lady, whosoever she may be."

"Sir Knight," replied the King, "gladly would I run a course with ye in honor of my lady. For I may tell ye she is a princess, and I do acclaim her as the most beautiful dame in all this world. But ere I take up your challenge, ye must needs agree to a condition: that he who is overthrown shall yield himself as a servant for seven days, and for that time he shall do all that his victor may require."

"Forsooth, 'tis a merry condition and full-heartedly do I accept your gage, Sir Unknown Knight," quoth Sir Geraint. "And when I have overthrown ye, ye will yield yourself up to those fair ladies to be their servant for seven days. And I do tell ye," said Sir Geraint with a twinkle in his eye, "that many a valiant knight would look on that as a pleasant and honorable task."

"Likewise," quoth King Arthur, "when ye are overthrown—for so ye shall be—I will send ye unto the service of my lady. And by my troth, that will be an even more pleasant and honorable task."

Whereupon each knight saluted the other and took his stand. And having made ready for the encounter, each shouted to his war horse and launched forth with great speed. So they met beneath the balcony, and each knight smote the other in the very center of his defense. And lo! the damsels overhead perceived how the spear of their champion burst into small pieces, but the spear of the stranger held. And Sir Geraint was overthrown so violently backward that both he and his horse were cast down to the ground, all in the gray dust.

Now so strongly had Sir Geraint been unseated that when he did recover his footing he was for some little while so astonished he knew not where he stood. Then coming quickly to himself again, he did draw his sword and he did call upon that stranger to leave his saddle and fight with him afoot.

But King Arthur said, "Nay, nay, Sir Knight. I have entirely overthrown thee. And as we did contract, thou art now pledged to be my servant."

Whereupon, though he was filled with shame and sorely vexed, Sir Geraint agreed to uphold his knightly word and he did put away his sword, saying, "I do acknowledge myself overthrown. Wherefore I yield myself to your command according to my plighted word." And then Sir Geraint knelt upon the ground, as if he were in truth naught but a lowly page.

And Arthur made reply, saying, "Rise, Sir Servant, and get thee straightway to Lady Guinevere at Cameliard. And do thou tell her that thou hast been overthrown by the knight that wore her necklace as a token, and that thou art come for to obey her in everything for seven days." And King Arthur laughed a glad and loving laugh, for truly he knew that knight for a loyal and honorable knight and he loved him well.

Then with knightly grace did Sir Geraint agree to the words of Arthur, whereupon he mounted his horse and turned toward Cameliard. And the King continued

on his way in high spirits toward the
place where he had seen the woodchoppers.

Now after King Arthur had traveled three leagues
more, he came upon a straight causeway that passed
through a stretch of marshland. And here were ditches
of water where the heron and the marsh-hen sought
harborage. Along the roadside were scattered numerous windmills, their sails turning slowly in the breeze.
And beside one windmill King Arthur did behold two
knights who sat upon their horses eating cheese and a
great loaf of bread.

Now both these knights were eager for adventure
on that summer's day, and when they did behold Ar-

thur, they straightway ceased eating and closed their helmets.

But Arthur perceived that those knights were his nephews, Sir Gawaine, the son of King Lot of Orkney, and Sir Ewaine, the son of King Urien of Gore. And Arthur knew Gawaine because on the crest of his helmet and eke upon his shield was engraven a device of a leopard rampant. And he knew that other knight to be Sir Ewaine because his crest did bear a unicorn upon it, and his shield did show a lady holding an unsheathed sword. Whereupon the King did close his helmet so that those two knights might not know him.

And as Arthur came nigh, Sir Gawaine rode forth and challenged him, saying, "Sir Knight, verily this is

King Arthur and Sir Geraint . . . launched forth with great speed.

perilous ground whereon ye have ventured. For there is no byway hence across the morass, nor may ye go forward without trying a tilt with me."

Unto this King Arthur did readily consent, on the condition that he who was overthrown would yield himself a servant for seven days. And gladly did Sir Gawaine accept this gage.

Whereupon each knight did take his station and did dress his spear and his shield. Then, shouting to his horse, each did rush forward unto the encounter. And each knight smote the other in the midst of his defense and lo! the spear of Gawaine splintered into fragments, but the spear of King Arthur did hold. And Sir Gawaine was lifted out of his saddle and over the crupper of his horse.

Now when Sir Gawaine rose up from the dust, the King said unto him, "Sir Knight and Servant, I have overthrown thee. Wherefore must thou obey me according to thy pledge."

"Not so!" cried Sir Ewaine, and straightway did he challenge the King to joust with him. "And furthermore," said he, "if I overthrow ye, ye must release my cousin from the servitude into which he is pledged. But if ye overthrow me, then likewise I will serve ye." Unto this, Arthur did readily agree.

So having made ready for the encounter, they met in that tilt like rams upon the hillside, and the King smote so strong a blow that the girths of Ewaine's saddle did verily burst apart, and both that saddle and that knight were cast down into the dust.

Then did King Arthur command those cousins to go to Cameliard and give service unto Lady Guinevere. And he bade them give her greeting from the White Champion that had received her necklace. Thus did Lady Guinevere get for servants two men, each the son of a king.

So did King Arthur continue on his way toward that place where he had seen the woodchoppers. And when he bethought himself on how those two good knights had fallen, and when he bethought himself on how they had been so abashed at their overthrow, he did laugh aloud for pure mirth, for never had he engaged in so joyous an adventure.

Now when he was within a league of his destination, he came upon a gnarled and stunted oak tree. And from that tree hung a shield of silver, and carven in that tree below that shield were these words:

WHOSO SMITETH UPON THIS SHIELD
DOETH SO AT THE PERIL OF HIS BODY.

Then did Arthur lift up his spear and he smote a heavy blow upon that shield.

And straightway came a voice from out of that forest, crying, "Who is it who dare assail my shield?"

Whereupon did ride forth a huge knight upon a

milk-white horse, and the trappings of that horse and of that knight were all white, like the trappings of the King. And that knight bore upon his helmet as his crest, a swan with outspread wings; and upon his shield were three swans a-swimming. Wherefore King Arthur knew that that knight was Sir Pellias who had come with him from Camelot to Tintagalon.

And Sir Pellias did take up his shield from off that tree, and he quoth, "Ho, Sir Knight. Prepare to defend yourself, for ye have struck my shield, as I did forbid."

Now for all his seeming sternness, Sir Pellias was very blithe at heart that a knight had taken up his challenge. For heretofore had been only idleness since he had come to Tintagalon, and now was he well pleased at this adventure. Wherefore he spurred his horse and started for his station.

But Arthur called after him, "Stay! Stay, Sir Knight! Ere I do combat, ye must contract that that knight who is overcome shall serve the other for the space of seven days."

And Sir Pellias did agree to that condition, whereupon each knight took his station and dressed his spear and shield. And when they had prepared themselves for the encounter, they burst forth like two stones cast from a catapult. So did they meet, and once again was Arthur the victor. For Sir Pellias was cast with passing violence out of his saddle, and for a considerable while did he lie quiet. And when he did recover, the King commanded him to go to Cameliard where he would do service unto the Lady Guinevere.

"Thither go I at your bidding," quoth Sir Pellias. "Yet ere I go, I would fain know who ye are, for never in all my life hath any knight overthrown me as ye have overthrown me."

Whereupon the King replied, "The time will come when thou shalt know who I am." And so saying, Arthur rode off.

So that day there came to Cameliard, first Sir Geraint, then Sir Gawaine and Sir Ewaine, and then Sir Pellias. And when these four beheld one another, they were all mightily abashed, albeit they were greatly cheered in spirit, each to find his own friends in like plight.

And the Lady Guinevere did greatly marvel, for it was passing strange and a thing unheard of that one knight, in one day, and with one spear, might overthrow five such knights as Duke Mordaunt, Sir Geraint, Sir Gawaine, Sir Ewaine, and Sir Pellias. And Guinevere was exceeding pleased that she had bestowed her necklace upon that champion, and blithe in spirit was she that he had brought honor upon her. And she did wonder mightily what manner of man her champion was. And betimes she mused he was a prince, and betimes she mused he was a high-born knight, yet never did that lady surmise that her champion was King of all the realm.

The Merriment
of Lady Guinevere

NOW THAT JOUST with Sir Pellias was verily the last
adventure that befell King Arthur on that day, and
soon did he come to that place where the woodchoppers worked, and there did he abide for that night.
Came the next morn, and Arthur did once again garb
himself in a jerkin of rough frieze. Then he did entrust those woodchoppers with the care of his horse
and of his armor, and he did promise them reward for
that service. Then turned he back to Cameliard. Soon
did he reach the edge of that forest, whereupon he set
his magic cap upon his head.

Now when Arthur came unto the castle grounds,
the chief gardener did greet him with exceeding wrath,
saying, "Knave! wherefore didst thou quit thy work to
go a-gadding?" And he took up a long birch rod with
which to punish that truant boy.

But Arthur laughed and said, "Touch me not!"

Whereupon the gardener caught the King by the
collar of his jerkin, saying, "Dost mock me, knave?
Now will I beat thee well for thy insolence."

Now heretofore Arthur had been content to play
the humble lad, but when he did feel that man's hand

upon his royal person, the King's spirit rose up within him, and he cried out, "Ha, wretch! how dost thou dare to lay thy hands upon me!" Then straightway did he wrench the rod from the gardener and he did strike him across the shoulders with it. "Now get thee gone and trouble me no more!" quoth the King.

Then straightway ran the gardener to the Lady Guinevere to complain that his boy had beaten him. But that lady only laughed, and she said, "Let him be, and meddle no more with him, for indeed, he is a very saucy fellow. But he is for me, and not for thee, to deal with."

Now indeed was Guinevere very merry, for she began to perceive wherefore it was that when the White Champion came forth, the gardener's boy departed, and when the White Champion departed, the gardener's boy came forth. For though for the most part she did rejoice that she had given her token to the White Champion, betimes she did lament not to have saved that token for that comely knight whom her leech had healed in the hermitage. Wherefore when she mused how, haply, these two knights might be one and the same, a great gladness fell upon her. Nor would she tell any of her ladies-in-waiting wherefore she smiled, though her maidens did beseech her to disclose to them the cause of her merriment.

Now that day in the afternoon, Guinevere did go a-walking in the garden with her maidens and with those four knights who had been sent thither by the White Champion. And as they passed the gardener's lad and saw him digging, the Lady Guinevere did laugh aloud as she called out, "Look! messires and ladies! Yonder is a very saucy fellow who continually doth wear his cap, even in the presence of lords and ladies."

Whereupon did Sir Gawaine speak and say, "Doth he so? Now will I take off that knave's cap for him."

"Let be, Sir Gawaine!" quoth Guinevere laughingly. "He doth assure us all that he hath an ugly place upon his head, so let him wear his cap."

In such manner was the Lady Guinevere pleased to make a mock of the King. And Arthur marked how high her spirits were, and in his heart was he pleased.

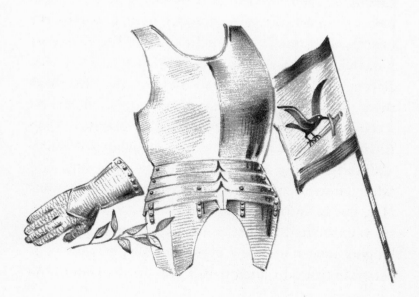

The Gardener's Boy
Goes Mad

NOW THIRTEEN days had King Arthur been at Cameliard. And each day had the sun risen brightly, nor had there been any clouds in that summer sky save such fleecy shimmerings as make, from time to time, a welcome shade. But on the fourteenth day those clouds grew dark, and the sky was overcast from end to end.

And on that day did Duke Mordaunt of North Umber recover entirely from those wounds that he had suffered at the hands of the White Champion. Wherefore he appeared again on the meadow before the castle, clad all in armor. And two heralds rode before him, winding loudly on their trumpets. And at that clarion, the lords and ladies of the court gathered upon the walls, and likewise came forth King Leodegrance.

Now when the Duke of North Umber beheld King Leodegrance, he cried out in a loud and rasping voice, "What ho! King Leodegrance! Thought ye that one fall from my horse was enough to get ye quit of me? Nay, not so. Wherefore shall I tomorrow return with six valiant knights-companion, and ye must pit seven knights against us. Now if your knights do prove our betters in the joust, then shall I give up all claim to the hand of the Lady Guinevere. But if ye have no such champions wherewith to defend your honor, then shall I claim the Lady Guinevere and those three castles of yours that stand nearest the borders of North Umber." Thereupon the two heralds blew their trumpets once more, and Duke Mordaunt did turn his horse about and away he rode.

And these words did put King Leodegrance in great sorrow, for knights like unto the White Champion had he none; and as for the White Champion, had he not departed?

And King Leodegrance grieved that King Arthur had not sent answer by the herald that had gone forth to Camelot full two weeks before. And he did bethink himself wherein he had offended his overlord, that he had not sent him succor in his need. Wherefore, melancholy in spirit and sick at heart, did that king go alone unto his chamber.

And the Lady Guinevere also was sore troubled, wherefore she went into her garden and she did accost those four knights who were pledged to serve her, saying, "Messires, I do command ye to take up this challenge of Duke Mordaunt. Wherefore must ye go forth tomorrow to meet this duke and his knights-companion in battle. Nor do I use ye rashly, for I perceive ye are puissant knights. Nor are there any save ye four to defend us against our enemies."

Whereupon quoth Sir Gawaine, "Not so, my lady!

We are pledged only unto your service, and not at all are we bound unto the service of your honored father. Nor have we any quarrel with Duke Mordaunt or with his knights-companion. For we are knights of the court of King Arthur, and we may not, save at his command, take upon us a foreign quarrel or render service to any other king."

Then did Guinevere fall into great choler, and she said with great heat, "Either, Sir Gawaine, thou art passing faithful to thy liege lord, or else thou fearest to meet this duke and his knights-companion."

Whereat Sir Gawaine cried out with great anger, "Were ye a knight, ye would think three times or four ere ye found courage to speak those words to me." Whereupon he arose and departed the room. And Guinevere did also repair to her bower, where she did weep much, both from sorrow and from anger.

Now all this while Arthur had been digging in the garden not far off, and he did overhear that quarrel. Wherefore he went up to the chief gardener, and taking that man by the collar of his coat, he said, "Sirrah! I have a command to set upon thee." Then did the King thrust his hand into the bosom of his jerkin and he brought forth that necklace of pearls that Guinevere had given him. And the King quoth, "Do thou take this necklace to thy mistress and say unto her that she is to send those four knights hither to serve me with food and drink from her own table. And say that she is to command those knights that, henceforth, they are my servants and not hers."

When the gardener did hear those words, he did verily believe that his lad had gone mad. "How now!" said he. "Dost thou account me as even the bigger fool than thyself to dare to say such words to Lady Guinevere?"

Whereupon the King replied, "Thou shalt do as I command. And if thou dare disobey me, then shalt thou suffer much for thy transgression. Be off!" And Arthur's voice and manner were so lordly withal, that that gardener did take up the string of pearls and did run forthwith to find his mistress, crying, "Lady! Lady! Certes, my lad hath assuredly gone mad!"

Sir Gardener's Boy

NOW WHEN LADY GUINEVERE heard the gardener's story, and when she got back that necklace that she had given to the White Champion, then she knew of a certainty that the White Champion and the knight of the hermitage and the gardener's boy were, all three, one and the same. Whereupon she was filled with exceeding joy and she both laughed and wept. So, betwixt her weeping and laughter, she went forth to her four pledged knights, and she said unto them:

"My lords, ye have all four broken my command, for when I bid ye take up my quarrel with Duke Mordaunt, ye would not do so. And thou, Sir Gawaine, hast moreover spoken such angry words as no servant should speak unto his mistress, nor certes any knight unto the daughter of a king. Wherefore, by way of penance, ye must needs take foods prepared from my table—meats and white bread, sweetmeats and red wine —and bring that food to my gardener's boy. And ye are all four to serve that food to him as though he were a royal knight. And when ye have served him, ye are to obey him in whatsoever he may ordain. And because ye took not my quarrel upon ye as true knights should,

I will have none of your service, but hereafter ye are to be the servants of that gardener's boy and not mine. Nor dare ye say me nay in any part of this, or I will know right well that ye intend not to keep your word that ye plighted to the White Champion when he overthrew ye in combat."

And then did the Lady Guinevere turn and did leave those knights with mouths agape; and as for herself, she did marvel that she had refrained in their presence from bursting into laughter.

And now those four knights were inflamed with indignation. Nor could they bear to look one upon the other, so abashed were they at the affront that had been put upon them.

Then spoke Sir Gawaine in high dudgeon, and his voice trembled with choler. "Messires, this lady hath wantonly affronted us, and now must we indeed serve this gardener's boy as she hath ordained. But mark ye, we are no longer her servants but we are his servants; wherefore we may serve that lad as seems befitting to us. Therefore when we have fulfilled that one command that she hath set, to wit, the feeding of that boy, then I vow that with my own hand I shall slay that scurvy fellow. And following that, I shall put his churlish head in a bag and send that bag to Lady Guinevere. So shall that proud lady receive as great an affront as she hath bestowed upon us."

And much cheered by Gawaine's words, the four

did seek out the steward of that castle, and they did get from him the finest of table services and the best of that food that was served at Guinevere's table. Whereupon they did go into the garden with that supper, and they did go to that gardener's boy, and they bade him sit down and dine. And each knight told his name, and to each the lad replied, "Verily that is the name that I had guessed for thee."

Then they waited on him as though he were some great lord. And indeed, he was the greatest lord in all that realm, but those knights knew not that.

And Sir Gawaine said unto him, "Eat well, sirrah! For thou shalt hardly have another meal upon this earth." And the lad replied, "That lieth unto a will other than thine. For I shall haply eat many meals after this one; and thou shalt haply serve at them, as thou servest me now."

And those knights were full amazed to perceive how little their words did dismay that lad.

And when he was done eating, the boy said unto them, "Messires, clothe yourselves in armor and do ye make ready to go abroad with me. And then go thou, Sir Gawaine, to the stable-keeper and have him make ready the Lady Guinevere's palfrey for me to ride upon. And bring that palfrey to the postern gate of this castle, where I shall meet ye four."

And Sir Gawaine said, "It shall be done. But when we ride forth from this castle, it shall prove for thee a

*Then they waited on him as though he were some
great lord.*

sorry journey, and haply it shall prove thy last."

And the lad replied, "Sir Gawaine, I think not."

Now when all five had met at the postern gate,
Arthur saw how those knights sat stock still upon their
horses, and he quoth, "Is this how ye serve me? Nay,
Sir Gawaine and Sir Ewaine, ye must come down and
hold my stirrup for me. And ye, Sir Geraint and Sir
Pellias, ye must come down and hold my palfrey whilst
I mount."

Then did those four knights get down from their
horses, and Sir Gawaine said, "Make the most of this
honor that we do thee, for thou hast but little longer to
enjoy it."

And the gardener's boy replied, "Methinks to enjoy
greater honor still, by and by."

So did they five ride forth from that place, and the
gardener's boy would not permit them to ride either
before him or beside him. Wherefore they must all
four ride behind him.

Now in time they came up to a dark and dismal
woodland. Then did Sir Gawaine ride forward, and he
said, "Sir Gardener's Boy, seest thou yonder woodland?
So soon as we ride into it, thou shalt die."

And the lad turned about in his saddle, and he said,
"Ha! Sir Gawaine! Wouldst thou ride forward when
I bid thee ride behind me?" And as he spoke, Arthur
took the cap from off his head and, lo! they all perceived that it was King Arthur who did ride with them,

and they could neither speak nor stir in their astonishment.

Wherefore King Arthur quoth, "How now, Sir Knights? Have ye no greeting for me? Certes, ye have served me this day with ill grace, and ye have been quick and ready with your tongues. Then wherefore is it that when I speak to ye now, ye deign me no reply?"

Then those four knights cried out aloud. And they leaped down from their horses, and they kneeled down in the dusty road. And when Arthur beheld them kneeling there, he stretched out his hands to them and bade them have good cheer.

Then he bade them mount their horses, and they rode away to the place of the woodchoppers, where the King had left his horse and his armor. And where the way was narrow King Arthur rode the foremost, but when the way was broad they all five rode abreast. And as they journeyed forward, Arthur did recount all his adventures, and they did learn how the King himself was the White Champion. And his knights-companion rejoiced greatly that come the morn, they would go forth with their liege lord to do battle with the enemies of King Leodegrance.

The Famous
Bout at Arms

CAME THE NEXT morn and the sun shone bright again, and the Duke of North Umber did appear as he had plighted, with six knights-companion on the field beside the castle of Cameliard. And behind those seven knights there rode seven esquires, and in front of them rode seven heralds with trumpets and tabards.

And the seven heralds blew their trumpets so loudly that all that town resounded with the blasts, and the people did come running unto that castle. Now Duke Mordaunt and his retinue did parade the length of that field beneath a cloudless sky, whilst that crowd did stand upon those walls and gaze down at that shining spectacle. And all the court of King Ryence did gather by that king's pavilion and they did shout and cheer the Duke of North Umber and his companions-at-arms.

But King Leodegrance was so low-spirited in his shame that he durst not show his face and kept away from that field, nor would he permit anyone of his court to come into his presence.

Wherefore the Lady Guinevere did go unto the apartments of that king and she did call unto her father through the door of his chamber, saying, "Lord King and father, look up, I prithee, and take good cheer unto thee. For there is one who hath our cause in hand, and he shall assuredly come ere this day is done. And when he cometh, he shall overthrow our enemies."

And King Leodegrance said to her from his chamber, "Thou sayest so but to comfort me. For even my overlord will not succor me, though I did send word of my need. Wherefore there is no one to help me in the hour of my trouble."

And she said, "Nay, I say truly to thee, the help that God shall send thee, he sendeth through a worthy champion who verily hath our cause in his hand." And though the King did not come forth, yet was he greatly comforted by the words of Guinevere.

And so passed that morning and so passed the better part of that afternoon, and no knightly company came forward to take up the challenge of Duke Mordaunt and his knights-companion.

Now when there were less than three hours ere the sun would set, the people of Cameliard, standing on the walls of that castle, did perceive at a great distance a cloud of dust. And encircled in that cloud were five knights who did ride forward in all haste. And with those five knights was a riderless palfrey. And when those knights drew nigh, that palfrey turned and made her way into the stables of Cameliard. And verily that horse was the palfrey of the Lady Guinevere.

And lo! the foremost of those five stalwart knights was indeed the White Champion who had overthrown Mordaunt of North Umber. And the four who did ride with him were Sir Ewaine, Sir Gawaine, Sir Geraint, and Sir Pellias, known to all throughout the realm as puissant men-at-arms. Wherefore did all that crowd cheer with a mighty voice.

Now when King Leodegrance heard the shouting of his people, hope rose within his breast, and forth he did come to see what was ado. Likewise did Guinevere come forth. And when she did behold the White Champion, then was her heart nigh to breaking with gladness, and withal, such was her excitement that she wept. And she waved her kerchief to that noble lord and to his companions, and she kissed her hand to them, and those five comely knights did salute her as they did ride out onto that field.

So soon as the Duke of North Umber perceived that the White Champion was the chiefest of those knights, he did ride up to him, saying, "A week past did I encounter ye, but for petty cause. Today's quarrel is more weighty than that other, wherefore will I not run a course with ye until I know who ye are. Now do I bid ye to declare what man ye are."

Then did Sir Gawaine open his visor and he quoth, "Know ye that I am Gawaine, the son of King Lot of Lothian and Orkney, of a condition and estate the equal of your own. And I do allege that yonder White Knight is of such quality that he doth indeed condescend to ye when he doth combat with ye, and that ye do not condescend to him."

"Ho, Sir Gawaine!" quoth the Duke. "I marvel at ye, for there are few men so exalted that they may condescend to me. But be that as it may, we may not fight with ye, for we are seven and ye are but five. And ye stand in great peril if ye undertake so unequal an encounter."

Then Sir Gawaine smiled, saying, "We thank ye for your compassion, good North Umber, and for the tender thoughts ye have for us. Yet we five perceive that it is ye seven, not ourselves, who stand in the greater peril."

Thereupon each knight spurred and turned his horse, and that party of seven did ride to one end of the field, and that party of five did ride to the other. And Arthur rode in the middle of his party, with two knights on both sides of his royal person. And in the other party did ride Duke Mordaunt in the middle, with three knights at either hand.

Then did Arthur and Mordaunt shout out, and each party did launch upon the other with such violence that the ground shuddered underfoot, and the dust rose up in clouds against the heavens.

And they met in the middle of the field in such uproar that the clash of swords and shields resounded even a mile away. And when the one party had passed the other, lo! three of those seven knights had been overthrown, but not one of that valiant five had lost his seat.

And one of the overthrown was Duke Mordaunt, nor did he ever rise from that ground whereon he lay. For Arthur had directed his spear into the very center of his defense, and the spear did hold fast, and the point thereof did pierce the shield of Mordaunt and his body armor. For so violent was that stroke that Mordaunt was verily lifted out of his saddle and he was cast a full spear's length behind the crupper of his horse. And as King Arthur turned to see how his enemy did fare, the evil soul quitted that body with a weak noise like the squeaking of a bat, and thus did that vainglorious man give up the ghost.

Now when the King beheld that but four knights remained of the seven, he did bestow upon his four knights great honor, bidding them to carry on that adventure by themselves, whilst he would retire from that fray and await the outcome thereof. So those four knights prepared for a new encounter, but Arthur sat quiet on his milk-white steed, and he looked upon that field with great contentment, ne'er doubting that his four valiant knights would win the day.

And the King did see how Sir Gawaine drove close to the foremost of his enemies, Sir Dinador of Mont-calm, of high renown. And when Sir Gawaine was in

reach of Sir Dinador, he did lift himself up in his stir-
rups and he did smite that knight so fierce a blow that
he verily cleft the shield and helmet of Sir Dinador,
leaving in that mighty stroke part of his own sword-
blade in Sir Dinador's helmet.

And with that puissant blow, the brains of Sir Dinador did swim like water, and the fear of death did fall
upon him. Whereupon he drew rein and fled away
from that field. And when his companions beheld how
he was struck and how he fled, they became disheart-
ened and turned craven and likewise fled.

Whereupon Sir Gawaine and Sir Ewaine and Sir
Geraint and Sir Pellias pursued those knights, and they·
chased them through the gathering that was the court

of King Ryence, so that the knights and nobles of that court were scattered hither and thither. And they did pursue those craven four among the pavilions and through the town and out across the moorlands. And when they returned from that chase, straightway they did go to where Arthur sat steadfast on his. horse, to do the King homage.

Whereupon the people of Cameliard did give up a mighty cheer, so loud and long that the reverberation of those joyful sounds did follow those five knights as they rode across field and drawbridge, and from thence into the town of Cameliard.

Thus ended that great bout-at-arms which was indeed one of the most renowned in chivalry.

And they met in the middle of the field

The Last Jest

NOW WHEN KING ARTHUR had come into the town of Cameliard, he left his knights-companion and straightway he did go unto that merchant, Ralph of Cardiff, to deliver back to him his sword and his armor and his milk-white horse. And the King quoth, "To-morrow shall ye receive two bags of gold for the rent of that armor that I got from ye."

And to this did Sir Ralph make reply, "My liege lord, it is not meet that ye should recompense me, for ye have this day rendered great honor unto Cameliard."

Whereupon Arthur said, "Have done, Sir Merchant. I am not such a man as ye may defy. Wherefore take ye whatsoever I shall send unto ye."

Thereupon he went his way on foot, and having set his magic cap upon his head, he came back into the gardens of the Lady Guinevere.

And when Guinevere beheld that gardener's boy again, she did laugh aloud and she did turn unto Sir Gawaine and unto Sir Ewaine, who were with her, saying, "Messires, behold! Yonder is that gardener's boy who weareth his cap continually because he hath an ugly place upon his head."

Now were those two knights exceedingly abashed at her speech. And Sir Gawaine did whisper in the ear of Sir Ewaine, "'Fore Heaven, that lady knoweth not what manner of man is yon gardener's boy, else would she be more sparing of her speech."

Now the Lady Guinevere did see Sir Gawaine speak, but she did not hear his words. So, turning to him, she said, "Sir Gawaine, if thou art affronted that yonder lad doth wear his cap before us, mayhap thou wilt go and take it off him as thou didst offer heretofore."

"Peace, Lady!" quoth Sir Gawaine. "Hadst thou more knowledge, thou wouldst not speak in this wise. For yonder gardener's boy could more easily take my head from off my shoulders than I could take that cap from off his head."

At this, Lady Guinevere made open laughter, but secretly did she ponder what Sir Gawaine meant by that saying. For though she knew that lad three times over—as gardener's lad and as the White Champion and as the knight of the hermitage—yet she guessed that there was still more to learn than met her eye.

Came the morn and the people of Cameliard looked over the castle walls and lo! they beheld that in the middle of that past night King Ryence had struck his pavilions and had departed. And with him had he taken the body of his cousin, Duke Mordaunt of North Umber. And the pages of King Ryence did carry off

that corpse in a satin litter, and they did walk along-
side it bearing lighted candles.

And the people of Cameliard were exceedingly rejoiced, and they made merry, and shouted and sang
and laughed.

It was about noon of that day when lo! there rode
up into the castle of Cameliard a herald from King
Ryence of North Wales, who strode into the hall up
to King Leodegrance, declaring: "My master, King
Ryence of North Wales, is greatly displeased with ye.
For ye have not rendered up to him those lands and
castles that border upon North Wales. And ye have
slain his cousin, Duke Mordaunt of North Umber, that
formerly was an excellent nobleman. Therefore my
master is affronted with ye beyond measure, nor will
he pardon ye but on two conditions: first, that straightway ye turn over those lands to him; and second, that
straightway ye deliver to him that White Knight who
slew the Duke of North Umber."

Then King Leodegrance arose from his seat, and he
quoth, "Sirrah, get thee gone, for thou and thy lord do
pass all bounds of insolence."

"Say you so?" said the herald. "Then will King
Ryence presently come hither with a great force of
arms. And he will take from ye by force those things
that ye might have delivered unto him peacefully."
So saying, the herald departed the hall.

Whereupon King Leodegrance did go into his

chamber, and he did command the presence of his daughter Guinevere. And he said to her, "Lady, twice hath a knight clad all in white come to our rescue and overthrown our enemies. Now it is said that this knight is thy champion, and that he wore thy necklace as a favor when first he did do battle with the Duke of North Umber. Wherefore I prithee tell me, who is that White Champion and where may he be found?"

Then the blood rushed from that lady's cheeks and she turned her head to hide her pallor, saying, "Verily, my lord, I know not who that knight may be."

Then did King Leodegrance take her hand in his, and he did bid her sit beside him, and he quoth, "Lady, thou art of an age to take to thee a man to cherish thee and to protect thee. For, lo! thou wert the child of my middle age and I grow old in years. Wherefore I may not always serve as thy protector. Moreover, my knights-at-arms are, for the most part, gone from me, for King Arthur hath brought peace to this realm, and all that noble court of chivalry which one time gathered about me is scattered elsewhere.

"Now meseems that of all the knights of chivalry, thou canst find thyself no better guardian than this White Knight. For indeed he is a mighty champion, such that only King Arthur could serve thee better. Wherefore it will be well if thou dost incline unto him, for methinks that he doth incline unto thee."

At this, the blood rushed back into her face and that

lady did blush a rosy red, and she did laugh until the tears flowed from her eyes and did run down her cheeks. And she said to King Leodegrance, "My lord and father, if I give up my affection to any man, I will give it to that poor boy who diggeth in my garden."

And greatly was the King angered at this lightness, and he cried out, "Ha, Lady! wouldst make a mock of me and a jest of my words?"

"Indeed, my lord," said Lady Guinevere, "I jest not and I mock not. For that gardener's boy is as dear to me as the White Champion. And if thou wouldst know more of this, then must thou learn it from the lad himself." And she fell to laughing again so heartily that she could not speak another word.

Whereupon the King bethought himself, saying, "Verily, there may be more in this matter than I perceive." And he dispatched a page to fetch that lad.

The Winning of a Queen

NOW WHEN THE gardener's lad appeared, with him came those four valiant knights of Camelot, to wit: Sir Gawaine, Sir Ewaine, Sir Geraint, and Sir Pellias. And those four lords did stand in attendance before Arthur at the door of the chamber of King Leodegrance. And the gardener's boy came forward to the table where the King sat with Lady Guinevere. And King Leodegrance did look upon that gardener's boy, and he said, "Ha! Wouldst wear thy cap in our presence?"

And the gardener's boy made reply, "I dare not take off my cap."

Whereupon King Leodegrance said, "Ha! Sayest thou? Now do I require thee to take off thy cap."

"Nay, my lord! Verily I dare not," quoth Arthur.

"How now!" cried out Leodegrance, "how darest thou flout my desire! Now do I command thee to take off thy cap."

And to this outburst Arthur did make no reply.

And then the Lady Guinevere spoke up, saying, "I do beseech thee, Messire, to take off thy cap unto my father."

Whereupon the gardener's boy did say, "At thy bidding, my fair lady, will I take it off." And so saying, Arthur did remove the magic cap from off his head.

Now when King Leodegrance saw who stood before him, he cried out, all in amazement, "My lord and my king! What is this?" Then he did rise from his seat and he did kneel down upon the floor, and he did clasp his hands, and he said, "My lord! My lord! Is it then thou who hast done all these wonders?"

"Yea," said King Arthur, "such as those things were, I have done them." And Arthur stooped and he kissed King Leodegrance upon the cheek, and he took that king's hands into his own. And he did lift Leodegrance up onto his feet, saying words of good cheer.

Now when the Lady Guinevere perceived that the White Champion was that man who was King of all the realm, she likewise was seized with amazement, and a great fear did fall upon her. And she did bethink herself, "How I have dallied with this King!" Said she unto herself, "And how I have made a jest of him who is greater even than my father ever was!" So whilst the two Kings gave royal greeting to one another, she did withdraw and did go and stand apart against the window, and she did tremble in her every limb.

Now when Arthur saw how she did stand far off by herself, he did straightway go to her and he did take her by the hand, saying, "Lady, what melancholy possesseth thee?"

And she made reply, "My lord, I am afeared of thy greatness."

Then quoth King Arthur, "Nay, my lady, it is rather I who am afeared of thee. For thy kind regard is dearer to me than all else in the world. Anything thou mightst command would I perform for the sake of thy good will."

And Guinevere said, "My liege lord, thou hast my good will."

And Arthur said, "Have I thy good will in great measure?"

"Yea," she replied, "thou hast it in great measure."

Whereupon he did bow his head and he did kiss her before all those who were there. And all that gathering was exceedingly delighted. And indeed King Leodegrance shed tears because of the great gladness that did possess him.

Thus was plighted the troth of King Arthur and the Lady Guinevere.

Lady Guinevere's Dowry

NOW PASSED THREE weeks after the betrothal of King Arthur and the Lady Guinevere, and there followed a great war with King Ryence of North Wales. And Sir Kay and Sir Ulfius had gathered a mighty army of men-at-arms as King Arthur had bidden them to do. Wherefore when King Ryence did come with his array against Cameliard, he was altogether routed and his army was dispersed. And King Ryence himself was pursued into the remotest mountains, and there dwelt he an outcast for the rest of his days.

Then was Cameliard filled with great rejoicing. And King Arthur did consent to stay in that castle for a month of days, and to that castle there repaired all the lords and ladies of King Arthur's court. Then followed feasts and jousts and many bouts-at-arms. And Arthur and Guinevere did prosper in spirit, and did enjoy that happy time together.

Now one day whilst Arthur sat at feast with Leodegrance and the enchanter Merlin, the old King said, "My liege lord, what shall I give thee for my daughter's dowry when thou takest her away to be thy Queen?"

Then Arthur did turn to Merlin, saying, "What shall I have from this noble knight for dowry?"

And that sage made reply, "Whatsoever thou dost want of him, will he give thee. Wouldst have wealth? King Leodegrance keepeth a full treasury."

"Nay," quoth King Arthur. "I have wealth enow."

"Wouldst have health? King Leodegrance hath in his court a marvelous physician."

"Nay," quoth King Arthur, "when I am sick, my lady-love will heal me."

"Or wouldst thou be such sort of King," quoth Merlin, "that the renown and the glory of thy reign shall never be forgotten?"

"Yea," quoth King Arthur, "I would fain be that King."

Whereupon Merlin said, "I will tell thee a story."

Then did Merlin speak at length in the presence of these two kings. And ere he was half done, Arthur was

glad at heart. And when he was all done, then was
King Arthur exceeding jubilant. And here followeth
the speech of Merlin unto those kings.

"In the days of thy father, Uther-Pendragon, I
caused to be made for him a certain table, and that
table was cut in the shape of a ring, wherefore men did
call it the Round Table. Now at this table are seats for
fifty men, and these men were to be those fifty knights
who were accounted as the most worthy knights in all
of Christendom. And whensoever a worthy knight
cometh to take his place, his name doth suddenly appear, writ all in gold, upon that seat destined for him.
And when that knight dieth, then doth his name vanish
altogether from that seat where he was wont to sit.

"Now, eight and forty of those seats are altogether
alike, and the forty-ninth seat is reserved for the King
of the realm, and that seat is elevated above all the
others. And all nine and forty seats are carven of ma-
hogany, and over each is spread a canopy of silk, sewed
with threads of linen."

"Now tell us of that fiftieth seat," said Arthur, in
impatience.

"Ah!" quoth Merlin, "that fiftieth seat is rightly
called the Seat Perilous. And, certes, that fiftieth seat
is more magnificent than any other, yea, even than the
seat of the King. For it is inset entire with gold and
silver, and it is covered with a canopy of satin embroidered all over with threads of silver and gold. And

never hath any name appeared upon the Seat Perilous, nor durst any knight sit there, save that one knight for whom it is intended. Wherefore should any other dare to sit there, either he dieth a sudden death, or else a great misfortune doth befall him. Wherefore is that seat called the Seat Perilous.

"Now in the days of Uther-Pendragon, there sat seven and thirty knights at the Round Table. And when Uther-Pendragon passed away, he gave that Round Table to his dearest friend, to wit: King Leodegrance of Cameliard. And in the beginning of the reign of Leodegrance, there sat four and twenty knights at the Round Table.

"But, alas! the times are changed, and the glory of this good king's reign hath paled before the glory of thy reign. Wherefore there now remaineth at that table not one name, save the name of Leodegrance himself. And that wondrous table doth lie beneath its pavilion in unseemly state.

"Now, wert thou to restore that table unto its rightful use and honor, it would lend unto thy reign its greatest glory. For I foresee that in thy day every seat of that table shall be filled, yea, even the Seat Perilous. And the fame of those knights who will sit around it shall never pass from the memory of man. Wherefore I counsel thee to ask that table of King Leodegrance, in dower for the Lady Guinevere."

Then quoth King Arthur to King Leodegrance, "My

teacher doth counsel me to ask of thee that Round Table of which he speaketh.''

And King Leodegrance said, "If that table bring thee glory, that glory shall be my glory, and thy renown will be mine. For if my glory waneth, and if thy glory increaseth, behold! is not my child thy wife? My liege lord, Arthur, the Table Round is thine, given to thee with all my heart.''

And thus did the Round Table come to the court of King Arthur, and it was set up at Camelot. And, by and by, there did gather about that table such an array of knights as the world had never before beheld and which it shall never behold again.

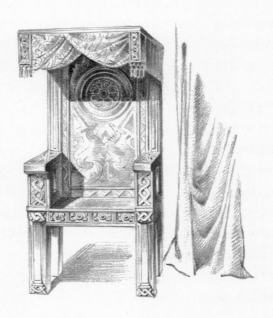

My Lord Doth Wed
his Lady

AND NOW WAS come the early fall of the year when the air is warm by day and cool by night, and the meadow is still green with summer. And the leaves of the trees are all gold and crimson, so that he who walks in the forest is verily under a beauteous canopy. And on a certain day in that autumn, banners were hung up in the town of Camelot, and the Lady Guinevere did journey unto that town from Cameliard. And with her came her father King Leodegrance, and a goodly retinue of lords and ladies, and seventeen noble knights that King Arthur had sent to her from Camelot for escort.

Now when King Arthur heard that she had come into the town of Camelot, he mounted on a roan-red stallion, and he hastened past the castle gates and rode out into the town. And all his company of lordly knights, save only those seventeen that had gone forth to Cameliard, did ride after the King.

Now when the two parties met, the noble Leodegrance did alight from his litter, whilst Arthur did dismount from his horse. Thereupon did Arthur give his bridle unto Sir Gawaine and Sir Ewaine, and alone went he forward to his lady's litter. Whereupon a page boy drew aside the silken curtains, and King Leodegrance gave his hand to Guinevere, and that lady was indeed exceeding beautiful in that hour. So did King Leodegrance bring her to stand before King Arthur. And Arthur placed one hand beneath her comely chin and the other upon the hair of her head, and he bowed his own head and he did kiss her on her cheek. Whereupon did all those assembled lift up their voices in acclaim.

Then did all that regal company go forward unto the castle of Camelot, wherein apartments were assigned to each according to his station, and joy filled that royal castle.

Came high noon, and all that court did repair with pomp and ceremony to the cathedral, wherein the nuptials of that noble lord, King Arthur, and his bride, Guinevere, were to be celebrated. And there did the Archbishop of Canterbury join those two noble souls as man and wife.

Then all the bells did ring out right joyfully, and all the folk gathered outside that cathedral did shout with loud acclaim. And, lo! King Arthur and Queen Guinevere came forth from the cathedral, the twain shining in their splendor like the midday sun.

And in the castle of Camelot, there was spread a great noontide feast. And thereat sat nigh to half a thousand high-born guests — kings and knights and nobles, queens and ladies, all in magnificent array. And at the table of the King and the Queen, were seated King Leodegrance, the father of the Queen, and Sir Ector the Trustworthy, the foster-father of the King, and Merlin the enchanter. And present in that hall were Sir Ulfius, and Sir Gawaine, and Sir Ewaine, and King Ban, and King Pellinore, and many other famous knights so that no man had ever beheld such a courtly company as was gathered there together at that great wedding-feast.

The Ancient and Honorable Companions

NOW WHEN THAT noble company had eaten and drunk to surfeit, the King and his Queen and all the court did go forward to that place where Merlin had caused to be built a wondrous pavilion wherein to house that Round Table that was the dowry of Guinevere.

And when that court did enter that pavilion, the surpassing beauty of that tabernacle did amaze each and every one for that pavilion did appear to be a marvelous land of faerie. For its walls were all richly gilded and upon them were painted the likenesses of saints and angels clad all in ultramarine and crimson, playing upon lutes and lyres and all manner of musical instruments. And the roof of that pavilion was like unto the sky, for it was bedaubed with cerulean blue sprinkled all over with stars. And in the middle of that roof was an image of the sun in all his glory. And the pavement underfoot was all of marble, cut in squares of black and white, and blue and red, and sundry other hues.

And in the center of that pavilion stood the Round Table, so ye might say it was the heart of that pavilion.

Now when the King and his court did enter, lo! of a
sudden sweet music was heard. And none could tell
who did play that melody, for indeed it was faerie song.
Whereupon Merlin did take King Arthur by the hand,
saying, "Lo! this is thy Round Table!"

Then Merlin led the King to that seat that was elevated above all others, saying, "This, my liege lord, is
the Seat Royal, and this seat is thine to sit in." And as
King Arthur did go forward to that seat, lo! there suddenly appeared upon its back, all writ in letters of gold,
the name

ARTHUR, KING

And Merlin said, "Yonder seat may well be called
the center seat of the Round Table, for that seat is
thine, and thou art indeed the very center of chivalry."

"Now," quoth the King, "thou must name me my
other knights. Thus let us in all haste find a sufficient
number to fill this Round Table, so that my glory shall
be complete."

Then Merlin smiled tenderly upon the King, and he
said, "Thou forgettest, King Arthur, the Seat Perilous,
where no man but one dare sit. And that man is not yet
born upon this earth.

"And wherefore is thy haste? For when this Round
Table is entirely filled, then shall thy glory be entirely
achieved. And then, alack! forthwith shall thy day be-
gin to decline, for when any man doth reach the height

of glory, his work is mostly done, and then God breaketh him as a man breaketh the chalice from which a noble toast is drunk, so that no baser usage may defile it. Thus when thy work is done shall God shatter the chalice of thy life."

Then did Arthur look steadfast upon the visage of his counselor, and he said, "My dear old friend, thy sayings are ever wise and wonderful to contemplate, and whatever thou dost not know, methinks no man can know. Yet since I am in God's hands, I do wish to see the speedy accomplishment of my glory, come what may."

"Thou hast a large and noble heart," quoth Merlin. "Wherefore thou speakest like a noble king. Yet may I not fill the Round Table for thee at this time. For though thou hast gathered all about thee the noblest court of chivalry in all of Christendom, yet there are but two and thirty knights here present who are worthy to sit at this Round Table."

"Then, Merlin," quoth the King, "do thou straightway choose me those two and thirty."

So Merlin cast his eyes around and, lo! he saw King Pellinore standing at a little distance. And Merlin did take King Pellinore by the hand, saying, "Here verily is the second worthiest knight in all this court. For he is gentle of demeanor, yet he is puissant and terrible in arms. And in all this court, none but King Arthur hath the skill to overthrow him. Yea, and if the King overthrow him on the one day, it may be on the next day that Pellinore will be the victor."

Then Merlin led King Pellinore forward and, behold! upon the seat that was at the left hand of the Seat Royal, there appeared in letters of gold the name,

PELLINORE

And when King Pellinore took his seat, great and loud acclaim was given him by all those who stood about.

And after Merlin had chosen King Arthur and King Pellinore, he chose out of the court another thirty knights, and all two and thirty were valiant in chivalry, and they were the first to establish the Round Table. Wherefore they were surnamed *"The Ancient and Honorable Companions of the Round Table."*

And among the thirty there were Sir Gawaine and Sir Ewaine, who were nephews unto the King, and Sir Ulfius and Sir Kay and Sir Geraint. And Sir Aglaval and Sir Lamorac and Sir Durnure, who were the sons of King Pellinore. And Sir Pellias and Sir Palomides and Sir Baudwain of Britain. And the name of each was written in gold upon the seat that belonged to him.

The Covenant of the Round Table

NOW WHEN ALL THE KNIGHTS had been chosen, King Arthur did note that the seat at the right hand of the Seat Royal had not been filled and that it bore no name upon it. And he said, "How is this, that the seat at my right hand hath not been filled?"

And Merlin replied, "My liege lord, a name shall be upon that seat in yet a little while. And he who shall sit there shall be the greatest knight in all the world until there cometh, in later years, that knight who will occupy the Seat Perilous. For he who shall sit at thy right hand shall exceed all other men in beauty and in strength and in knightly grace. Wherefore he will be acclaimed as the greatest knight of this time and in worthiness he will be second only to thyself."

Whereupon King Arthur said, "I wish he were with us now."

And Merlin answered him in this way, "Patience, my lord, he cometh anon." And Merlin smiled right kindly on the King, for he knew that that knight who even now was on his way to Camelot, was none other than Sir Lancelot of the Lake.

Then was the Round Table established with great pomp and ceremony. And first the Archbishop of Canterbury blessed each and every seat, while the pages of his Holy Court did swing censers of sweet-smelling frankincense, and his choir sang glad psalms and hymns of joy.

And when each seat was blessed, each chosen knight sat in his place at the Round Table, and his esquire stood behind him, holding aloft the banneret of his lord. And all those who stood about that place, both knights and ladies, lifted up their voices in loud acclaim.

Then all the knights arose, and each knight lifted up his sword before him. And King Arthur did proclaim the covenant of the Knighthood of the Round Table, and each knight spoke it word for word.

And this is that covenant: That they would be gentle unto the weak; that they would be courageous unto the strong; that they would be terrible unto the wicked and the evil-doer; that they would defend the helpless who should call upon them for aid; that all women should be held sacred with them; that they would stand unto the defense of one another whensoever such defense should be required; that they would be merciful unto all men; that they would be gentle in deed, true in friendship, and faithful in love.

This, then, was the covenant, and unto it each knight did swear upon the cross of his sword. And

each knight kissed the hilt to seal that oath. And once more all that company that were witnesses thereof gave up a great shout.

And thus between one rising and one setting of the sun, did King Arthur wed his lady love, and he and Merlin did establish the Round Table. And the Round Table became the crowning achievement of King Arthur's reign, for about it there sat the finest knights in

...each knight lifted up his sword before him.

all the world, the full flower of chivalry. And those noble knights held King Arthur to be the very fountainhead of honor. And to the greater glory of King Arthur did that exalted brotherhood venture forth to do battle with the evils of this world.

And those adventures that befell the knights of the Round Table have also been set in a book, wherein ye may read anon.

HART

PUBLISHING

COMPANY